KT-140-459

THE WATER BABIES

To Rossanna.
With much love
and best wishes for Christmas 1986.
Aunt Sylvia.

The Water Babies

by

CHARLES KINGSLEY

illustrated by

HAROLD JONES

the text specially prepared by

KATHLEEN LINES

LONDON
VICTOR GOLLANCZ LTD
1985

This edition
© Victor Gollancz Ltd 1961
and
© Franklin Watts Inc. 1961

ISBN 0 575 00259 X

First published in 1961
by Victor Gollancz Ltd,
14 Henrietta Street, London WC2E 8QJ
Second impression 1969
Third impression January 1974
Fourth impression February 1976
Fifth impression June 1978
Sixth impression September 1980
Seventh impression February 1983
Eighth impression August 1985

Printed in Great Britain
by St Edmundsbury Press Ltd., Bury St Edmunds, Suffolk

To
My Youngest Son
Grenville Arthur
And To
All Other Good Little Boys

Come read my riddle, each good little man:
If you cannot read it, no grown-up folk can.

CHAPTER I

CHAPTER I

ONCE UPON A TIME there was a little chimney-sweep and
his name was Tom. He lived in a great town in the North country,
where there were plenty of chimneys to sweep, and plenty of
money for Tom to earn and his master to spend. He could not
read nor write, and did not care to do either; and he never washed
himself, for there was no water up the court where he lived. He
had never been taught to say his prayers. He never had heard of
God, except in words which it would have been well if he had
never heard. He cried half his time, and laughed the other half.
He cried when he had to climb the dark flues, rubbing his poor
knees and elbows raw; and when the soot got into his eyes, which
it did every day in the week; and when his master beat him, which
he did every day in the week; and when he had not enough to eat,
which happened every day in the week likewise. And he laughed
the other half of the day, when he was tossing half-pennies with
the other boys, or playing leap-frog over the posts, or bowling
stones at the horses' legs as they trotted by, which last was excellent
fun, when there was a wall at hand behind which to hide. As for
chimney-sweeping, and being hungry, and being beaten, he took
all that for the way of the world, like the rain and snow and
thunder, and stood manfully with his back to it till it was over, as
the old donkey did to a hailstorm; and then shook his ears and

was as jolly as ever; and thought of the fine times coming, when
he would be a man, and a master sweep, and sit in the public-
house with a quart of beer and a long pipe, and play cards for
silver money, and wear velveteens and ankle-jacks, and keep a
white bull-dog with one grey ear, and carry her puppies in his
pocket, just like a man. And he would have apprentices, one, two,
three, if he could. How he would bully them, and knock them
about, just as his master did to him; and make them carry
home the soot-sacks, while he rode before them on his donkey,
with a pipe in his mouth and a flower in his button-hole,
like a king at the head of his army. Yes, there were good
times coming; and, when his master let him have a pull at the
leavings of his beer, Tom was the jolliest boy in the whole
town.

One day a smart little groom rode into the court where Tom
lived. Tom was just hiding behind a wall, to heave half a brick at
his horse's legs, as is the custom of that country when they welcome strangers; but the groom saw him, and halloed to him
to know where Mr. Grimes, the chimney-sweep, lived. Now,
Mr. Grimes was Tom's own master, and Tom was a good
man of business, and always civil to customers, so he put the
half-brick down quietly behind the wall, and proceeded to take
orders.

Mr. Grimes was to come up next morning to Sir John Harthover's, at the Place, for his old chimney-sweep was gone to prison,
and the chimneys wanted sweeping. And so he rode away, not
giving Tom time to ask what the sweep had gone to prison for,

which was a matter of interest to Tom, as he had been in prison once or twice himself. Moreover, the groom looked so very neat and clean, with his drab gaiters, drab breeches, drab jacket, snow-white tie with a smart pin in it, and clean round ruddy face, that Tom was offended and disgusted at his appearance, and considered him a stuck-up fellow, who gave himself airs because he wore smart clothes, and other people paid for them; and went behind the wall to fetch the half-brick after all: but did not, remembering that he had come in the way of business, and was, as it were, under a flag of truce.

His master was so delighted at his new customer that he knocked Tom down out of hand, and drank more beer that night than he usually did in two, in order to be sure of getting up in time next morning; for the more a man's head aches when he wakes, the more glad he is to turn out, and have a breath of fresh air. And, when he did get up at four the next morning, he knocked Tom down again, in order to teach him (as young gentlemen used to be taught at public schools) that he must be an extra good boy that day, as they were going to a very great house, and might make a very good thing of it, if they could but give satisfaction.

And Tom thought so likewise, and, indeed, would have done and behaved his best, even without being knocked down. For, of all places upon earth, Harthover Place (which he had never seen) was the most wonderful; and, of all men on earth, Sir John (whom he had seen, having been sent to gaol by him twice) was the most awful.

Harthover Place was really a grand place, even for the rich North country; with a house so large that in the frame-breaking riots, which Tom could just remember, the Duke of Wellington, with ten thousand soldiers and cannon to match, were easily housed therein; at least, so Tom believed; with a park full of deer, which Tom believed to be monsters who were in the habit of eating children; with miles of game-preserves, in which Mr. Grimes and the collier lads poached at times, on which occasions Tom saw pheasants, and wondered what they tasted like; with a noble salmon-river, in which Mr. Grimes and his friends would have liked to poach; but then they must have got into cold water, and that they did not like at all. In short, Harthover was a grand place, and Sir John a grand old man, whom even Mr. Grimes respected, for not only could he send Mr. Grimes to prison when he deserved it, as he did once or twice a week; not only did he own all the land about for miles; not only was he a jolly, honest,

sensible squire as ever kept a pack of hounds, who would do
what he thought right by his neighbours, as well as get what he
thought right for himself, but, what was more, he weighed full
fifteen stone, was nobody knew how many inches round the chest,
and could have thrashed Mr. Grimes himself in fair fight, which
very few folk round there could do. So Mr. Grimes touched
his hat to him when he rode through the town, and called
him a "buirdly awd chap," and his young ladies "gradely
lasses," which are two high compliments in the North country;
and thought that that made up for his poaching Sir John's
pheasants.

Now, I dare say, you never got up at three o'clock on a midsummer morning. Some people get up then because they want to
catch salmon; and some, because they want to climb Alps; and a
great many more, because they must, like Tom. But, I assure you,
that three o'clock on a midsummer morning is the pleasantest
time of all the twenty-four hours, and all the three hundred and
sixty-five days; and why every one does not get up then, I never
could tell, save that they are all determined to spoil their nerves
and their complexions, by doing all night, what they might just
as well do all day. But Tom, instead of going out to dinner at half-
past eight at night, and to a ball at ten, and finishing off somewhere
between twelve and four, went to bed at seven, when his master
went to the public-house, and slept like a dead pig: for which
reason he was as pert as a game-cock, and just ready to get
up when the fine gentlemen and ladies were just ready to go to
bed.

So he and his master set out; Grimes rode the donkey in front, and Tom and the brushes walked behind; out of the court, and up the street, past the closed window-shutters, and the winking weary policemen, and the roofs all shining grey in the grey dawn.

They passed through the pitmen's village, all shut up and silent now; and through the turnpike; and then they were out in the real country, and plodding along the black dusty road, between black slag walls, with no sound but the groaning and thumping of the pit-engine in the next field. But soon the road grew white, and the walls likewise; and at the wall's foot grew long grass and gay flowers, all drenched with dew; and instead of the groaning of the pit-engine, they heard the skylark saying his matins high up in the air, and the pit-bird warbling in the sedges, as he had warbled all night long.

All else was silent, for old Mrs. Earth was still fast asleep. The great elm-trees in the gold-green meadows were fast asleep above, and the cows fast asleep beneath them; nay, the few clouds which were about were fast asleep likewise, and so tired that they had lain down on the earth to rest, in long white flakes and bars, among the stems of the elm-trees, and along the tops of the alders by the stream, waiting for the sun to bid them rise and go about their days' business in the clear blue overhead.

On they went; and Tom looked, and looked, for he never had been so far into the country before; and longed to get over a gate, and pick buttercups, and look for birds' nests in the hedge; but Mr. Grimes was a man of business, and would not have heard of that.

Soon they came up with a poor Irishwoman, trudging along with a bundle at her back, and wearing a grey shawl over her head, and a crimson petticoat. She had neither shoes nor stockings, and limped along as if she were tired and footsore: but she was a very tall handsome woman, with bright grey eyes, and heavy black hair hanging about her cheeks. And she took Mr. Grimes's fancy so much, that when he came alongside he called out to her:

"This is a hard road for a gradely foot like that. Will ye up, lass, and ride behind me?"

But, perhaps, she did not admire Mr. Grimes's look and voice; for she answered quietly:

"No, thank you; I'd sooner walk with your little lad here."

"You may please yourself," growled Grimes, and went on smoking.

So she walked beside Tom, and talked to him, and asked him where he lived, and what he knew, and all about himself, till Tom thought he had never met such a pleasant-spoken woman. And she asked him, at last, whether he said his prayers; and seemed sad when he told her that he knew no prayers to say.

Then he asked her where she lived; and she said far away by the sea. And Tom asked her about the sea; and she told him how it rolled and roared over the rocks in winter nights, and lay still in the bright summer days, for the children to bathe and play in it; and many a story more, till Tom longed to go and see the sea, and bathe in it likewise.

At last, at the bottom of a hill, they came to a spring: a real North country limestone fountain, like one of those in Sicily or Greece, where the old heathen fancied the nymphs sat cooling themselves the hot summer's day, while the shepherds peeped at them from behind the bushes. Out of a low cave of rock, at the foot of a limestone crag, the great fountain rose, quelling and bubbling and gurgling, so clear that you could not tell where the water ended and the air began; and ran away under the road, a stream large enough to turn a mill; among blue geranium, and golden globe-flower, and wild raspberry, and the bird-cherry with its tassels of snow.

And there Grimes stopped, and looked; and Tom looked too. Tom was wondering whether anything lived in that dark cave, and came out at night to fly in the meadows. But Grimes was not wondering at all. Without a word, he got off his donkey, and clambered over the low road wall, and knelt down, and began dipping his ugly head into the spring—and very dirty he made it.

Tom was picking the flowers as fast as he could. The Irish-woman helped him, and showed him how to tie them up; and a very pretty nosegay they had made between them. But when he saw Grimes actually wash, he stopped, quite astonished; and when Grimes had finished, and began shaking his ears to dry them, he said:

"Why, master, I never saw you do that before."

"Nor will again, most likely. 'Twasn't for cleanliness I did it, but for coolness. I'd be ashamed to want washing every week or so, like any smutty collier lad."

"I wish I might go and dip my head in," said poor little Tom. "It must be as good as putting it under the town-pump; and there is no beadle here to drive a chap away."

"Thou come along," said Grimes, "what dost want with washing thyself? Thou did not drink half a gallon of beer last night, like me."

"I don't care for you," said naughty Tom, and ran down to the stream, and began washing his face.

Grimes was very sulky, because the woman preferred Tom's company to his; so he dashed at him with horrid words, and tore him up from his knees, and began beating him. But Tom was accustomed to that, and got his head safe between Mr. Grimes's legs, and kicked his shins with all his might.

"Are you not ashamed of yourself, Thomas Grimes?" cried the Irishwoman over the wall.

Grimes looked up, startled at her knowing his name; but all he answered was, "No: nor never was yet;" and went on beating Tom.

"True for you. If you ever had been ashamed of yourself, you would have gone over into Vendale long ago."

"What do you know about Vendale?" shouted Grimes; but he left off beating Tom.

"I know about Vendale, and about you, too. I know, for instance, what happened in Aldermire Copse, by night, two years ago come Martinmas."

"You do?" shouted Grimes; and leaving Tom, climbed up over the wall, and faced the woman. Tom thought he was going to strike her; but she looked him too full and fierce in the face for that.

"Yes; I was there," said the Irishwoman, quietly.

"You are no Irishwoman, by your speech," said Grimes, after many bad words.

"Never mind who I am. I saw what I saw; and if you strike that boy again, I can tell what I know."

Grimes seemed quite cowed, and got on his donkey without another word.

"Stop!" said the Irishwoman. "I have one more word for you both; for you will both see me again, before all is over. Those that wish to be clean, clean they will be; and those that wish to be foul, foul they will be. Remember."

And she turned away, and through a gate into the meadow. Grimes stood still a moment, like a man who had been stunned.

Then he rushed after her, shouting "You come back." But when
he got into the meadow the woman was not there.

Had she hidden away? There was no place to hide in. But
Grimes looked about, and Tom also, for he was as puzzled as
Grimes himself, at her disappearing so suddenly; but look where
they would, she was not there.

Grimes came back again, as silent as a post, for he was a little
frightened; and getting on his donkey, filled a fresh pipe, and
smoked away, leaving Tom in peace.

And now they had gone three miles and more, and came to
Sir John's lodge-gates.

Very grand lodges they were, with very grand iron gates, and
stone gate-posts, and on the top of each a most dreadful bogy,
all teeth, horns, and tail, which was the crest which Sir John's
ancestors wore in the Wars of the Roses.

Grimes rang at the gate, and out came a keeper on the spot, and opened.

"I was told to expect thee," he said. "Now, thou'lt be so good as to keep to the main avenue, and not let me find a hare or a rabbit on thee when thou comest back. I shall look sharp for one, I tell thee."

"Not if it's in the bottom of the soot-bag," quoth Grimes, and at that he laughed; and the keeper laughed and said:

"If that's thy sort, I may as well walk up with thee to the hall."

"I think thou best had. It's thy business to see after thy game, man, and not mine."

So the keeper went with them; and to Tom's surprise, he and Grimes chatted together all the way quite pleasantly. He did not know that a keeper is only a poacher turned outside in, and a poacher a keeper turned inside out.

They walked up a great lime-avenue, a full mile long, and between their stems Tom peeped trembling at the horns of the sleeping deer, which stood up among the ferns. Tom had never seen such enormous trees, and as he looked up he fancied that the blue sky rested on their heads. But he was puzzled very much by a strange murmuring noise, which followed them all the way. So much puzzled, that at last he took courage to ask the keeper what it was.

He spoke very civilly, and called him Sir, for he was horribly afraid of him, which pleased the keeper, and he told him that they were the bees about the lime-flowers.

"What are bees?" asked Tom.

"What make honey."

"What is honey?" asked Tom.

"Thou hold thy noise," said Grimes.

"Let the boy be," said the keeper. "He's a civil young chap now, and that's more than he'll be long, if he bides with thee."

Grimes laughed, for he took that for a compliment.

"I wish I were a keeper," said Tom, "to live in such a beautiful place, and wear green velveteens, and have a real dog-whistle at my button, like you."

The keeper laughed; he was a kind-hearted fellow enough.

"Let well alone, lad, and ill too, at times. Thy life's safer than mine at all events, eh, Mr. Grimes?"

And Grimes laughed again, and then the two men began talking quite low. Tom could hear, though, that it was about some poaching fight; and at last Grimes said surlily:

"Hast thou anything against me?"

"Not now."

"Then don't ask me any questions till thou hast, for I am a man of honour."

And at that they both laughed again, and thought it a very good joke.

And by this time they were come up to the great iron gates in front of the house; and Tom stared through them at the rhododendrons and azaleas, which were all in flower; and then at the house itself, and wondered how many chimneys there were in it, and how long ago it was built, and what was the man's name that built it, and whether he got much money for his job?

These last were very difficult questions to answer. For Harthover had been built at ninety different times, and in nineteen different styles, and looked as if somebody had built a whole street of houses of every imaginable shape, and then stirred them together with a spoon.

So that Harthover house was a great puzzle to antiquarians, and to critics, and architects, who all set upon poor Sir John, year after year, and tried to talk him into spending a hundred thousand pounds or so, in building to please them and not himself. But he always put them off, like a canny North-countryman as he was. One wanted him to build a Gothic house, but he said he was no Goth; and another to build an Elizabethan, but he said he lived under good Queen Victoria, and not good Queen Bess; and another was bold enough to tell him that his house was ugly, but he said he lived inside it, and not outside; and another, that there was no unity in it; but he said that that was just why he liked the old place. For he liked to see how each Sir John, and Sir Hugh, and Sir Ralph, and Sir Randal, had left his mark upon the place, each after his own taste; and he had no more notion of disturbing his ancestors' work than of disturbing their graves. For now the house looked like a real live house, that had a history, and had grown and grown as the world grew; and that it was only an upstart fellow who did not know who his own grandfather was, who would change it for some spick and span new Gothic or Elizabethan thing, which looked as if it had been all spawned in a night, as mushrooms are. From which you may collect (if you have wit enough), that Sir John was a very sound-headed, sound-hearted squire, and just the man to keep the country-side in order, and show good sport with his hounds.

But Tom and his master did not go in through the great iron gates, as if they had been Dukes or Bishops, but round the back way, and a very long way round it was; and into a little back-door, where the ash-boy let them in, yawning horribly; and then in a passage the housekeeper met them, in such a flowered chintz dressing-gown, that Tom mistook her for My Lady herself, and she gave Grimes solemn orders about "You will take care of this, and take care of that," as if he was going up the chimneys, and not Tom. And Grimes listened, and said every now and then, under his voice, "You'll mind that, you little beggar?" and Tom did mind, all at least that he could. And then the housekeeper turned them into a grand room, all covered up in sheets of brown paper, and bade them begin, in a lofty and tremendous voice; and so after a whimper or two, and a kick from his master, into the grate Tom went, and up the chimney, while a housemaid stayed in the room to watch the furniture; to whom Mr. Grimes paid many playful and chivalrous compliments, but met with very slight encouragement in return.

Tom swept so many chimneys that he got quite tired, and puzzled too, for they were not like the town flues to which he was accustomed, but large and crooked chimneys, which had been altered again and again, till they ran into one another. So Tom fairly lost his way in them; not that he cared much for that, though he was in pitchy darkness, for he was as much at home in a chimney as a mole is underground; but at last, coming down

as he thought the right chimney, he came down the wrong one,
and found himself standing on the hearthrug in a room the like of
which he had never seen before.

Tom had never seen the like. He had only been in gentlefolks'
rooms when the carpets were all up, and the curtains down, and
the furniture huddled together under a cloth, and the pictures
covered with aprons and dusters; and he had often enough wondered what the rooms were like when they were all ready for the
quality to sit in. And now he saw, and he thought the sight very
pretty.

The room was all dressed in white; white window curtains,
white bed curtains, white furniture, and white walls, with
just a few lines of pink here and there. The carpet was all over
gay little flowers; and the walls were hung with pictures in
gilt frames, which amused Tom very much. There were
pictures of ladies and gentlemen, and pictures of horses and
dogs. The horses he liked; but the dogs he did not care for
much, for there were no bull-dogs among them, not even a
terrier. But the picture which took his fancy most, was one of a
man in long garments, with little children and their mothers
round him, who was laying his hand upon the children's heads.
That was a very pretty picture, Tom thought, to hang in a
lady's room. For he could see that it was a lady's room by the
dresses which lay about.

The other picture was that of a man nailed to a cross, which
surprised Tom much. He fancied that he had seen something like
it in a shop window. But why was it there? "Poor man," thought

Tom, "and he looks so kind and quiet. But why should the lady have such a sad picture as that in her room? Perhaps it was some kinsman of hers, who had been murdered by the savages in foreign parts, and she kept it there for a remembrance." And Tom felt sad, and awed, and turned to look at something else.

The next thing he saw, and that puzzled him, was a washing-stand, with ewers and basins, and soap and brushes, and towels; and a large bath, full of clean water—what a heap of things all for washing! "She must be a very dirty lady," thought Tom, "by my master's rule, to want as much scrubbing as all that. But she must be very cunning to put the dirt out of the way so well afterwards, for I don't see a speck about the room, not even on the very towels."

And then, looking toward the bed, he saw that dirty lady, and held his breath with astonishment.

Under the snow-white coverlet, upon the snow-white pillow, lay the most beautiful little girl that Tom had ever seen. Her cheeks were almost as white as the pillow, and her hair was like threads of gold spread all about over the bed. She might have been as old as Tom, or maybe a year or two older; but Tom did not think of that. He thought only of her delicate skin and golden hair, and wondered whether she were a real live person, or one of the wax dolls he had seen in the shops. But when he saw her breathe, he made up his mind that she was alive, and stood staring at her, as if she had been an angel out of heaven.

No. She cannot be dirty. She never could have been dirty, thought Tom to himself. And then he thought, "And are all people like that when they are washed?" And he looked at his own wrist, and tried to rub the soot off, and wondered whether it ever would come off.

And looking round, he suddenly saw, standing close to him, a little ugly, black, ragged figure, with bleared eyes and grinning white teeth. He turned on it angrily. What did such a little black ape want in that sweet young lady's room? And behold, it was himself, reflected in a great mirror, the like of which Tom had never seen before.

And Tom, for the first time in his life, found out that he was dirty; and burst into tears with shame and anger and turned to sneak up the chimney again and hide, and upset the fender, and threw the fire-irons down, with a noise as of ten thousand tin kettles tied to ten thousand mad dogs' tails.

Up jumped the little white lady in her bed, and, seeing Tom, screamed as shrill as any peacock. In rushed a stout old nurse from the next room, and seeing Tom likewise, made up her mind that he had come to rob, plunder, destroy, and burn; and dashed at him, as he lay over the fender, so fast that she caught him by the jacket.

But she did not hold him. Tom had been in a policeman's hands many a time, and out of them too, what is more; and he would have been ashamed to face his friends for ever if he had been stupid enough to be caught by an old woman: so he doubled under the good lady's arm, across the room, and out of the window in a moment.

He did not need to drop out, though he would have done so bravely enough. Nor even to let himself down the drain-pipe, which would have been an old game to him. But all under the window spread a tree, with great leaves, and sweet white flowers, almost as big as his head. It was a magnolia; but Tom knew nothing about that, and cared less; for down the tree he went like a cat, and across the garden lawn, and over the iron-railings, and up the park towards the wood, leaving the old nurse to scream murder and fire at the window.

The under-gardener, mowing, saw Tom, and threw down his scythe; caught his leg in it, and cut his shin open, whereby he kept to his bed for a week: but in his hurry he never knew it, and gave chase to poor Tom. The dairymaid heard the noise, got the churn between her knees, and tumbled over it, spilling all the cream; and yet she jumped up, and gave chase to Tom. A groom cleaning Sir John's hack at the stables let him go loose (whereby he kicked himself lame in five minutes) and ran out, and gave chase to Tom. Grimes upset the soot-sack in the new-gravelled

yard, and spoilt it all utterly; but, he ran out and gave chase to
Tom. The old steward opened the park gate in a hurry, and gave
chase to Tom. The ploughman left his horses at the headland, and
one jumped over the fence, and pulled the other into the ditch
plough and all; but he ran on, and gave chase to Tom. The keeper,
who was taking a stoat out of a trap, let the stoat go, and caught
his own finger; but he jumped up and ran after Tom, and con-
sidering what he said, and how he looked, I should have been
sorry for Tom if he had caught him. Sir John looked
out of his study window (for he was an early
old gentleman), and up at the nurse, and a martin
dropped mud in his eye, so that he had later to
send for the doctor; and yet he ran out
and gave chase to Tom. The Irishwoman,
too, was walking up to the house to
beg—she must have got round by some
byway: but she threw away her bundle, and
gave chase to Tom likewise. Only My Lady
did not give chase; for when she had put
her head out of the window, her night-wig
fell into the garden, and she had to ring

up her lady's-maid, and send her down for it privately; which quite put her out of the running.

In a word, never was there heard at Harthover Place, not even when the fox was killed in the conservatory, among acres of broken glass, and tons of smashed flower-pots, such a noise, row, hubbub, babel, shindy, hullabaloo, stramash, charivari, and total contempt of dignity, repose, and order, as that day, when Grimes, the gardener, the groom, the dairymaid, Sir John, the steward, the ploughman, the keeper, and the Irishwoman, all ran up the park, shouting "Stop thief," in the belief that Tom had at least a thousand pounds' worth of jewels in his empty pockets; and the very magpies and jays followed Tom up, screaking and screaming, as if he were a hunted fox, beginning to droop his brush.

And all the while poor Tom padded up the park with his little bare feet, like a small black gorilla fleeing to the forest. For Tom, of course, made for the woods, He had never been in a wood in his life: but he was sharp enough to know that he might hide in a bush, or swarm up a tree, and, altogether, had more chance there than in the open. If he had not known that, he would have been foolisher than a mouse or a minnow.

But when he got into the wood, he found it a very different sort of place from what he had fancied. He pushed into a thick cover of rhododendrons, and found himself at once caught in a trap. The boughs laid hold of his legs and arms, poked him in his face and his stomach, made him shut his eyes tight (though that was no great loss, for he could not see at best a yard before his nose); and when he got through the rhododendrons, the hassock-grass and sedges tumbled him over, and cut his poor little fingers afterwards most spitefully.

"I must get out of this," thought Tom, "or I shall stay here till somebody comes to help me—which is just what I don't want."

But how to get out was the difficult matter. And he might never have got out at all, but stayed there till the cock-robins covered him with leaves, if he had not suddenly run his head against a wall.

Now running your head against a wall is not pleasant, and Tom hurt his head; but he was a brave boy, and did not mind that a penny. He guessed that over the wall the cover would end; and up it he went, and over like a squirrel.

And there he was, out on the great grouse-moors, which the country folk called Harthover Fell—heather and bog and rock, stretching away and up, up to the very sky.

Now, Tom was a cunning little fellow—as cunning as an old Exmoor stag. Why not? Though he was but ten years old, he had lived longer than most stags, and had more wits to start with into the bargain.

He knew as well as a stag, that if he backed he might throw the hounds out. So the first thing he did when he was over the wall, was to make the neatest double sharp to his right, and run along under the wall for nearly half a mile.

Whereby Sir John, and the keeper, and the steward, and the gardener, and the ploughman, and the dairymaid, and all the hue-and-cry together, went on ahead half a mile in the very opposite direction, and inside the wall, leaving him a mile off on the outside, while Tom heard their shouts die away in the wood, and chuckled to himself merrily.

At last he came to a dip in the land, and went to the bottom of it, and then he turned bravely away from the wall, and up the moor; for he knew that he had put a hill between him and his enemies, and could go on without their seeing him.

But the Irishwoman, alone of them all, had seen which way Tom went. She had kept ahead of every one the whole time: and yet she neither walked nor ran. She went along quite smoothly and gracefully, while her feet twinkled past each other so fast, that you could not see which was foremost; till every one asked the other who the strange woman was; and all agreed, for want of anything better to say, that she must be in league with Tom.

But when she came to the plantation they lost sight of her; and they could do no less. For she went quietly over the wall after Tom, and followed him wherever he went. Sir John and the rest saw no more of her; and out of sight was out of mind.

And now Tom was right away into the heather, over the moor; and as he went upwards, it grew more and more broken and hilly: but not so rough but that little Tom could jog along well enough, and find time, too, to stare about at the strange place, which was like a new world to him.

He saw great spiders there, with crowns and crosses marked on their backs, who sat in the middle of their webs, and when they saw Tom coming, shook them so fast that they became invisible. Then he saw lizards, brown, and grey, and green, and thought they were snakes, and would sting him: but they were as much frightened as he, and shot away into the heath. And then, under a rock, he saw a pretty sight—a great brown, sharp-nosed creature, with a white tag to her brush, and round her, four or five smutty little cubs, the funniest fellows Tom ever saw. She lay on her back rolling about, and stretching out her legs, and head, and tail in the bright sunshine; and the cubs jumped over her, and ran round her, and nibbled her paws, and lugged her about by the tail; and she seemed to enjoy it mightily. But one selfish little fellow stole away from the rest to a dead crow close by, and dragged it off to hide it, though it was nearly as big as he was. Whereat all his little brothers set off after him in full cry, and saw Tom; and then all ran back, and up jumped Mrs. Vixen, and caught one up in her mouth, and the rest toddled after her, and into a dark crack in the rocks; and there was an end of the show.

And next he had a fright; for as he scrambled up a sandy brow—whirr-poof-poof-cock-cock-kick—something went off in his face, with a most horrid noise. He thought the ground had blown up, and the end of the world come.

And when he opened his eyes (for he shut them very tight) it was only an old cock-grouse, who had been washing himself in sand, like an Arab, for want of water; and who, when Tom had all but trodden on him, jumped up, with a noise like the express train, leaving his wife and children to shift for themselves, like an old coward, and went off, screaming "Cur-ru-u-uck, cur-ru-u-uck —murder, thieves, fire—cur-u-uck-cock-kick—the end of the world is come—kick-kick-cock-kick."

So Tom went on, and on, he hardly knew why: but he liked the great, wide, strange place, and the cool, fresh, bracing air. But he went more and more slowly as he got higher up the hill; for now the ground grew very bad indeed. Instead of soft turf and springy heather, he met great patches of flat limestone rock, just like ill-made pavements, with deep cracks between the stones and ledges, filled with ferns; so he had to hop from stone to stone, and now and then he slipped in between, and hurt his bare toes,

though they were tolerably tough ones: but still he would go on
and up, he could not tell why.

What would Tom have said, if he had seen, walking over the
moor behind him, the very same Irishwoman who had taken
his part upon the road? But whether it was that he looked too
little behind him, or whether it was that she kept out of sight
behind the rocks and knolls, he never saw her, though she
saw him.

And now he began to get a little hungry, and very thirsty;
for he had run a long way, and the sun had risen high in
heaven, and the rock was as hot as an oven, and the air danced
reels over it, as it does over a limekiln, till everything round
seemed quivering and melting in the glare.

But he could see nothing to eat anywhere, and still less to drink.

The heath was full of bilberries and whimberries: but they were
only in flower yet, for it was June. And as for water, who can find
that on the top of a limestone rock? Now and then he passed by a
deep dark swallow-hole, going
down into the earth, as if it was
the chimney of some dwarf's
house underground; and more
than once, as he passed, he
could hear water falling, trick-
ling, tinkling, many many feet
below. How he longed to get
down to it, and cool his poor
baked lips! But, brave little

chimney-sweep as he was, he dared not climb down such chimneys as those.

So he went on, and on, till his head spun round with the heat, and he thought he heard church-bells ringing, a long way off.

"Ah!" he thought, "where there is a church, there will be houses and people; and, perhaps, some one will give me a bit and a sup." So he set off again, to look for the church; for he was sure that he heard the bells quite plain.

And in a minute more, when he looked round, he stopped again, and said, "Why, what a big place the world is!"

And so it was; for, from the top of the mountain, he could see—what could he not see?

Behind him, far below, was Harthover, and the dark woods, and the shining salmon-river; and on his left, far below, was the town, and the smoking chimneys of the collieries; and far, far away, the river widened to the shining sea; and little white specks, which were ships, lay on its bosom. Before him lay, spread out like a map, great plains, and farms, and villages, amid dark knots of trees. They all seemed at his very feet; but he had sense to see that they were long miles away.

And to his right rose moor after moor, hill after hill, till they faded away, blue into blue sky. But between him and those moors, and really at his very feet, lay something, to which, as soon as Tom saw it, he determined to go, for that was the place for him.

A deep, deep green and rocky valley, very narrow, and filled with wood: but through the wood, hundreds of feet below him, he could see a clear stream glance. Oh, if he could but get down to that stream! Then, by the stream, he saw the roof of a little cottage, and a little garden, set out in squares and beds. And there was a tiny little red thing moving in the garden, no bigger than a fly. As Tom looked down, he saw that it was a woman in a red petticoat! Ah! perhaps she would give him something to eat. And there were the church-bells ringing again. Surely there must be a village down there. Well, nobody would know him, or what had happened at the Place. The news could not have got there yet, even if Sir John had set all the policemen in the county after him; and he could get down there in five minutes.

Tom was quite right about the hue-and-cry not having got thither; for he had come, without knowing it, the best part of ten miles from Harthover: but he was wrong about getting down in five minutes, for the cottage was more than a mile off, and a good thousand feet below.

However, down he went, like the brave little man he was, though he was very footsore, and tired, and hungry, and thirsty; while the church-bells rang so loud, he began to think that they must be inside his own head, and the river chimed and tinkled far below; and this was the song which it sang:

Clear and cool, clear and cool,
By laughing shallow, and dreaming pool,
Cool and clear, cool and clear,
By shining shingle, and foaming wear;
Under the crag where the ouzel sings,
And the ivied wall where the church-bell rings,
Undefiled, for the undefiled;
Play by me, bathe in me, mother and child.

Dank and foul, dank and foul,
By the smoky town in its murky cowl;
Foul and dank, foul and dank,
By wharf and sewer and slimy bank;
Darker and darker the further I go,
Baser and baser the richer I grow;
Who dare sport with the sin-defiled?
Shrink from me, turn from me, mother and child.

Strong and free, strong and free,
The floodgates are open, away to the sea.
Free and strong, free and strong,
Cleansing my streams as I hurry along,
To the golden sands, and the leaping bar,
And the taintless tide that awaits me afar,
As I lose myself in the infinite main,
Like a soul that has sinned and is pardoned again.
Undefiled, for the undefiled,
Play by me, bathe in me, mother and child.

So Tom went down; and all the while he never saw the Irish-woman going down behind him.

CHAPTER II

CHAPTER II

A MILE OFF, and a thousand feet down. So Tom found it; though it seemed as if he could have chucked a pebble on to the back of the woman in the red petticoat who was weeding in the garden, or even across the dale to the rocks beyond.

For the bottom of the valley was just one field broad, and on the other side ran the stream; and above it, grey crag, grey down, grey stair, grey moor, walled up to heaven.

A quiet, silent, rich, happy place is Vendale; a narrow crack cut deep into the earth; so deep, and so out of the way, that the bad bogies can hardly find it out.

So Tom went to go down; and first he went down three hundred feet of steep heather, mixed up with loose brown gritstone, as rough as a file; which was not pleasant to his poor heels, as he came bump, stump, jump, down the steep. And still he thought he could throw a stone into the garden.

Then he went down three hundred feet of limestone terraces, one below the other, as straight as if they had been ruled with a ruler and then cut out with a chisel. There was no heath there, but—

First, a little grass-slope, covered with the prettiest flowers; rockrose and saxifrage, and thyme and basil, and all sorts of sweet herbs.

Then bump down a two-foot step of limestone.

Then another bit of grass and flowers.

Then bump down a one-foot step.

Then another bit of grass and flowers for fifty yards, as steep as the house-roof, where he had to sit down and slide.

Then another step of stone, ten feet high; and there he had to stop himself, and crawl along the edge to find a crack; for if he had rolled over, he would have rolled right into the old woman's garden, and frightened her out of her wits.

Then, when he had found a dark narrow crack, full of green-stalked fern, and had crawled down through it, with knees and elbows, as he would down a chimney, there was another grass-slope, and another step, and so on and on.

At last he came to a bank of beautiful shrubs; white beam with its great silver-backed leaves, and mountain-ash, and oak; and below them cliff and crag, cliff and crag, with great beds of crown-ferns and wood-sedge; while through the shrubs he could see the stream sparkling, and hear it murmur on the white pebbles. He did not know that it was still three hundred feet below.

You would have been giddy, perhaps, at looking down: but Tom was not. He was a brave little chimney-sweep; and when he found himself on the top of this high cliff, he said, "Ah, this will just suit me!" though he was very tired; and down he went, by stock and stone, sedge and ledge, bush and rush, as if he had been born a jolly little black ape, with four hands instead of two.

And all the while, he never saw the Irishwoman coming down behind him.

But he was getting terribly tired now. The burning sun on the fells had sucked him up; but the damp heat of the woody crag sucked him up still more; and the perspiration ran out of the ends of his fingers and toes, and washed him cleaner than he had been for a whole year. But, of course, he dirtied everything terribly as he went. There has been a great black smudge all down the crag ever since.

At last he got to the bottom. But, behold, it was not the bottom —as people usually find when they are coming down a mountain. For at the foot of the crag were heaps and heaps of fallen limestone of every size from that of your head to that of a stage-waggon, with holes between them full of sweet heath-fern; and before Tom got through them, he was out in the bright sunshine again; and then he felt, once for all and suddenly, as people generally do, that he was b-e-a-t, beat.

He could not get on. He lay down on the grass. The sun was burning, and yet he felt chill all over. He was quite empty, and yet he felt quite sick. There was but two hundred yards of smooth pasture between him and the cottage, and yet he could not walk down it. He could hear the stream murmuring only one field beyond it, and yet it seemed to him as if it was a hundred miles off.

He lay on the grass till the beetles ran over him, and the flies settled on his nose. I don't know when he would have got up again, if the gnats and the midges had not taken compassion on him. But the gnats blew their trumpets so loud in his ear, and the midges nibbled so at his hands and face wherever they could find a place free from soot, that at last he woke up, and stumbled

away, down over a low wall, and into a narrow road, and up to
the cottage door.

And a neat pretty cottage it was, with clipped yew hedges all
round the garden, and yews inside too, cut into peacocks and
trumpets and teapots and all kinds of queer shapes. And out of the
open door came a noise like that of the frogs when they know that
it is going to be scorching hot to-morrow—and how they know
that I don't know, and you don't know, and nobody knows.

He came slowly up to the open door, which was all hung
round with clematis and roses; and then peeped in, half afraid.

And there sat by the empty fire-place, which was filled with a pot of sweet herbs, the nicest old woman that ever was seen, in her red petticoat, and short dimity gown, and clean white cap, with a black silk handkerchief over it, tied under her chin. At her feet sat the grandfather of all the cats; and opposite her sat, on two benches, twelve or fourteen neat rosy chubby little children, learning their Chris-cross-row; and gabble enough they made about it.

Such a pleasant cottage it was, with a shiny clean stone floor, and curious old prints on the walls, and an old black oak sideboard full of bright pewter and brass dishes, and a cuckoo clock in the corner, which began shouting as soon as Tom appeared: not that it was frightened by Tom, but that it was just eleven o'clock.

All the children started at Tom's dirty black figure; the girls began to cry, and the boys began to laugh, and all pointed at him rudely enough: but Tom was too tired to care for that.

"What art thou, and what dost want?" cried the old dame. "A chimney-sweep! Away with thee. I'll have no sweeps here."

"Water," said poor little Tom, quite faint.

"Water? There's plenty i' the beck," she said, quite sharply.

"But I can't get there; I'm most clemmed with hunger and drought." And Tom sank down upon the door-step, and laid his head against the post.

And the old dame looked at him through her spectacles one minute, and two, and three; and then she said, "He's sick; and a bairn's a bairn, sweep or none."

"Water," said Tom.

"God forgive me!" and she put by her spectacles, and rose, and came to Tom. "Water's bad for thee; I'll give thee milk," And she toddled off into the next room, and brought a cup of milk and a bit of bread.

Tom drank the milk off at one draught, and then looked up, revived.

"Where didst come from?" said the dame.

"Over Fell, there," said Tom, and pointed up into the sky.

"Over Harthover? and down Lewthwaite Crag? Art sure thou art not lying?"

"Why should I?" said Tom, and leant his head against the post.

"And how got ye up there?"

"I came over from the Place," and Tom was so tired and desperate he had no heart or time to think of a story, so he told all the truth in a few words.

"Bless thy little heart! And thou hast not been stealing, then?"

"No."

"Bless thy little heart! and I'll warrant not. Why, God's guided the bairn, because he was innocent! Away from the Place, and over Harthover Fell, and down Lewthwaite Crag! Who ever heard the like, if God hadn't led him? Why dost not eat thy bread?"

"I can't."

"It's good enough, for I made it myself."

"I can't," said Tom, and he laid his head on his knees, and then asked:

"Is it Sunday?"

"No, then; why should it be?"

"Because I hear the church-bells ringing so."

"Bless thy pretty heart! The bairn's sick. Come wi' me, and I'll hap thee up somewhere. If thou wert a bit cleaner I'd put thee in my own bed, for the Lord's sake. But come along here."

But when Tom tried to get up, he was so tired and giddy that she had to help him and lead him.

She put him in an outhouse upon soft sweet hay and an old rug, and bade him sleep off his walk, and she would come to him when school was over, in an hour's time.

And so she went in again, expecting Tom to fall fast asleep at once.

But Tom did not fall asleep.

Instead of it he turned and tossed and kicked about in the strangest way, and felt so hot all over that he longed to get into the river and cool himself; and then he fell half asleep, and dreamed that he heard the little white lady crying to him, "Oh, you're so dirty; go and be washed"; and then that he heard the Irishwoman saying, "Those that wish to be clean, clean they will be." And then he heard the church-bells ring so loud, close to him, too, that he was sure it must be Sunday, in spite of what the old dame had said; and he would go to church, and see what a church was like inside, for he had never been in one, poor little fellow, in all his life. But the people would never let him come in, all over soot and dirt like that. He must go to the river and wash first. And he said out aloud again and again, though being half asleep he did not know it, "I must be clean, I must be clean."

And all of a sudden he found himself, not in the outhouse on the hay, but in the middle of a meadow, over the road, with a stream just before him, saying continually, "I must be clean, I must be clean." He had got there on his own legs, between sleep and awake, as children will often get out of bed, and go about the room, when they are not quite well. But he was not a bit surprised, and went on to the bank of the brook, and lay down on the grass, and looked into the clear, clear limestone water, with every pebble at the bottom bright and clean, while the little silver trout dashed about in fright at the sight of his black face; and he dipped his hand in and found it so cool, cool, cool; and he said, "I will be a fish; I will swim in the water; I must be clean, I must be clean."

So he pulled off all his clothes in such haste that he tore some of them, which was easy enough with such ragged old things. And he put his poor hot sore feet into the water; and then his legs; and the further he went in, the more the church-bells rang in his head.

"Ah," said Tom, "I must be quick and wash myself; the bells are ringing quite loud now: and they will stop soon, and then the door will be shut, and I shall never be able to get in at all."

And all the while he never saw the Irish woman: not behind him this time, but before.

For just before he came to the river side, she had stepped down into the cool clear water; and her shawl and her petticoat floated off her, and the green water-weeds floated round her sides, and the white waterlilies floated round her head, and the fairies of the stream came up from the bottom, and bore her away and down upon their arms; for she was the Queen of them all; and perhaps of more besides.

"Where have you been?" they asked her.

"I have been smoothing sick folk's pillows, and whispering sweet dreams into their ears; opening cottage casements, to let out the stifling air; coaxing little children away from gutters, and foul pools where fever breeds; turning women from the gin-shop door, and staying men's hands as they were going to strike their wives; doing all I can to help those who will not help themselves: and little enough that is, and weary work for me. But I have brought you a new little brother, and watched him safe all the way here."

Then all the fairies laughed for joy at the thought that they had a little brother coming.

"But mind, maidens, he must not see you, or know that you are here. He is but a savage now, and like the beasts which perish; and from the beasts which perish he must learn. So you must not play with him, or speak to him, or let him see you; but only keep him from being harmed."

Then the fairies were sad, because they could not play with their new brother, but they always did what they were told.

And their Queen floated away down the river; and whither she went, thither she came. But all this Tom, of course, never saw or heard: and perhaps if he had, it would have made little difference in the story; for he was so hot and thirsty, and longed so to be clean for once, that he tumbled himself as quick as he could into the clear cool stream.

And he had not been in it two minutes before he fell fast asleep, into the quietest, sunniest, cosiest sleep that ever he had in his life; and he dreamed about the green meadows by which he had walked that morning, and the tall elm-trees, and the sleeping cows; and after that he dreamed of nothing at all.

The reason of his falling into such a delightful sleep is very simple; and yet hardly any one has found it out. It was merely that the fairies took him.

The kind old dame came back at twelve, when school was over, to look at Tom: but there was no Tom there. She looked about for his footprints; but the ground was so hard that there was no slot, as they say in North Devon.

So the old dame went in again quite sulky, thinking that little Tom had tricked her with a false story, and shammed ill, and then run away again.

But she altered her mind the next day. For, when Sir John and the rest of them had run themselves out of breath, and lost Tom, they went back again, looking very foolish.

And they looked more foolish still when Sir John heard more of the story from the nurse; and more foolish still, again, when they heard the whole story from Miss Ellie, the little lady in white. All she had seen was a poor little black chimney-sweep, crying and sobbing, and going to get up the chimney again. Of course, she was very much frightened: and no wonder. But that was all. The boy had taken nothing in the room; by the mark of his little sooty feet, they could see that he had never been off the hearth-rug till the nurse caught hold of him. It was all a mistake.

So Sir John told Grimes to go home, and promised him five shillings if he would bring the boy quietly up to him, without beating him, that he might be sure of the truth. For he took for granted, and Grimes, too, that Tom had made his way home.

But no Tom came back to Mr. Grimes that evening; and he went to the police-office, to tell them to look out for the boy. But no Tom was heard of. As for his having gone over those great fells to Vendale, they no more dreamed of that than of his having gone to the moon.

So Mr. Grimes came up to Harthover next day with a very sour face; but when he got there, Sir John was over the hills and far away; and Mr. Grimes had to sit in the outer servants' hall all day, and drink strong ale to wash away his sorrows; and they were washed away, long before Sir John came back.

For good Sir John had slept very badly that night; and he said to his lady, "My dear, the boy must have got over into the grouse-moors, and lost himself; and he lies very heavily on my conscience, poor little lad. But I know what I will do."

So, at five the next morning up he got, and into his bath, and into his shooting-jacket and gaiters, and into the stable-yard, like a fine old English gentleman, with a face as red as a rose, and a hand as hard as a table, and a back as broad as a bullock's; and bade them bring his shooting pony, and the keeper to come on his pony, and the huntsman, and the first whip, and the second whip, and the under-keeper with the bloodhound in a leash—a great dog as tall as a calf, of the colour of a gravel walk, with mahogany ears and nose, and a throat like a church-bell. They took him up to the place where Tom had gone into the wood; and there the hound lifted up his mighty voice, and told them all he knew.

Then he took them to the place where Tom had climbed the wall; and they shoved it down, and all got through.

And then the wise dog took them over the moor, and over the fells, step by step, very slowly; for the scent was a day old, you know, and very light from the heat and drought. But that was why cunning old Sir John started at five in the morning.

And at last he came to the top of Lewthwaite Crag, and there he bayed, and looked up in their faces, as much as to say, "I tell you he is gone down here!"

They could hardly believe that Tom would have gone so far; and when they looked at that awful cliff, they could never believe that he would have dared to face it. But if the dog said so, it must be true.

"Heaven forgive us!" said Sir John. "If we find him at all, we shall find him lying at the bottom." And he slapped his great hand upon his great thigh, and said:

"Who will go down over Lewthwaite Crag, and see if that boy is alive? Oh that I were twenty years younger, and I would go down myself!" And so he would have done, as well as any sweep in the county. Then he said:

"Twenty pounds to the man who brings me that boy alive!" and as was his way, what he said he meant.

Now among the lot was a little groom-boy, a very little groom indeed; and he was the same who had ridden up the court, and told Tom to come to the Hall; and he said:

"Twenty pounds or none, I will go down over Lewthwaite Crag, if it's only for the poor boy's sake. For he was as civil a spoken little chap as ever climbed a flue."

So down over Lewthwaite Crag he went: a very smart groom he was at the top, and a very shabby one at the bottom; for he tore his gaiters, and he tore his breeches, and he tore his jacket, and he burst his braces, and he burst his boots, and he lost his hat, and what was worst of all, he lost his shirt pin, which he prized very much, for it was gold, and he had won it in a raffle, so it was a really severe loss: but he never saw anything of Tom.

And all the while Sir John and the rest were riding round, full three miles to the right, and back again, to get into Vendale, and to the foot of the crag.

When they came to the old dame's school, all the children came out to see. And the old dame came out too; and when she saw Sir John she curtsied very low, for she was a tenant of his.

"Well, dame, and how are you?" said Sir John.

"Blessings on you as broad as your back, Harthover," says she— she didn't call him Sir John, but only Harthover, for that is the fashion in the North country—"and welcome into Vendale: but you're no hunting the fox this time of year?"

"I am hunting, and strange game too," said he.

"Blessings on your heart, and what makes you look so sad the morn?"

"I'm looking for a lost child, a chimney-sweep, that is run away."

"Oh, Harthover, Harthover," says she, "ye were always a just man and a merciful; and ye'll no harm the poor little lad if I give you tidings of him?"

"Not I, not I, dame. I'm afraid we hunted him out of the house all on a miserable mistake, and the hound has brought him to the top of Lewthwaite Crag, and——"

Whereat the old dame broke out crying, without letting him finish his story.

"So he told me the truth after all, poor little dear! Ah, first thoughts are best, and a body's heart'll guide them right, if they will but hearken to it." And then she told Sir John all.

"Bring the dog here, and lay him on," said Sir John, without another word, and he set his teeth very hard.

And the dog opened at once; and went away at the back of the cottage, over the road, and over the meadow, and through a bit of alder copse; and there, upon an alder stump, they saw Tom's clothes lying. And then they knew as much about it all as there was any need to know.

And Tom?

Ah, now comes the most wonderful part of this wonderful story. Tom, when he woke, for of course he woke—children always wake after they have slept exactly as long as is good for them—found himself swimming about in the stream, being about four inches, or—that I may be accurate—3·87902 inches long, and having round his neck a set of external gills just like those of a sucking eft, which he mistook for a lace frill, till he pulled at them, found he hurt himself, and made up his mind that they were part of himself, and best left alone.

In fact, the fairies had turned him into a water-baby.

A water-baby? You never heard of a water-baby. Perhaps not. There are a great many things in the world which you never heard of; and a great many more which nobody ever heard of; and a great many things, too, which nobody will ever hear of, at least until the coming of the Cocqcigrues, when man shall be the measure of all things."

"But there are no such things as water-babies."

How do you know that? Have you been there to see? And if you had been there to see, and had seen none, that would not prove that there were none. And no one has a right to say that no water-babies exist, till they have seen no water-babies existing; which is quite a different thing, mind, from not seeing water-babies; and a thing which nobody ever did, or perhaps ever will do.

"But surely if there were water-babies, somebody would have caught one at least?"

Well. How do you know that somebody has not?

"But a water-baby is contrary to nature."

You must not say that this cannot be, or that that is contrary to nature. You do not know what nature is, or what she can do. Wise men are afraid to say that there is anything contrary to nature, except what is contrary to mathematical truth; for two and two cannot make five, and two straight lines cannot join twice, and a part cannot be as great as the whole, and so on (at least, so it seems at present): but the wiser men are, the less they talk about "cannot." That is a very rash, dangerous word, that "cannot"; and if people use it too often, the Queen of all the Fairies, who makes the clouds thunder and the fleas bite, and takes just as much trouble about one as about the other, is apt to astonish them suddenly by showing them, that though they say she cannot, yet she can, and what is more, will, whether they approve or not.

And therefore it is, that there are dozens and hundreds of things in the world which we should certainly have said were contrary to nature, if we did not see them going on under our eyes all day long. If people had never seen little seeds grow into great plants and trees, of quite different shape from themselves, and these trees again produce fresh seeds, to grow into fresh trees, they would have said, "The thing cannot be; it is contrary to nature." And they would have been quite as right in saying so, as in saying that most other things cannot be.

Did not learned men, too, hold, till within the last twenty-five years, that a flying dragon was an impossible monster? And do we not know now that hundreds of them have been found as fossils up and down the world? People call them Pterodactyls: but that is only because they are ashamed to call them flying dragons, after denying so long that flying dragons could exist.

The truth is, that folks' fancy that such and such things cannot be, simply because they have not seen them, is worth no more than a savage's fancy that there cannot be such a thing as a loco-motive, because he never saw one running wild in the forest. Wise men know that their business is to examine what is, and not to settle what is not. They know that there are elephants; they know that there have been flying dragons; and the wiser they are, the less inclined they will be to say positively that there are no water-babies.

No water-babies, indeed? Why, wise men of old said that every-thing on earth had its double in the water; and you may see that that is, if not quite true, still quite as true as most other theories which you are likely to hear for many a day. There are land-babies —then why not water-babies? Are there not water-rats, water-flies, water-crickets, water-crabs, water-tortoises, water-scorpions, water-tigers and water-hogs, water-cats and water-dogs, sea-lions and sea-bears, sea-horses and sea-elephants, sea-mice and sea-urchins, sea-razors and sea-pens, sea-combs and sea-fans; and of plants, are there not water-grass, and water-crowfoot, water-milfoil, and so on, without end?

But at all events, so it happened to Tom. And, therefore, the keeper, and the groom, and Sir John, made a great mistake, and were very unhappy (Sir John, at least) without any reason, when they found a black thing in the water, and said it was Tom's body, and that he had been drowned. They were utterly mistaken. Tom was quite alive; and cleaner, and merrier, than he ever had been. The fairies had washed him, you see, in the swift river, so thoroughly, that not only his dirt, but his whole husk and shell had been washed quite off him, and the pretty little real Tom was washed out of the inside of it, and swam away, as a caddis-worm does when its case of stones and silk is bored through, and away it goes on its back, paddling to the shore, there to split its skin, and fly away as a caperer, on four fawn-coloured wings, with long legs and horns.

But good Sir John did not know all this, and he took it into his head that Tom was drowned. When they looked into the empty pockets of his clothes, and found no jewels nor money—nothing but three marbles, and a brass button with a string to it—then Sir John did something as like crying as ever he did in his life, and blamed himself more bitterly than he need have done. So he cried, and the groom-boy cried, and the huntsman cried, and the dame cried, and the little girl cried, and the dairymaid cried, and the old nurse cried (for it was somewhat her fault), and My Lady cried, but the keeper did not cry, though he had been so good-natured to Tom the morning before; for he was so dried up with running after poachers, that you could no more get tears out of him than milk out of leather: and Grimes did not cry, for Sir John gave him ten pounds, and he drank it all in a week. Sir John sent, far and wide, to find Tom's father and mother; but he might have looked till Doomsday for them, for one was dead, and the other had been transported to Botany Bay. And the little girl would not play with her dolls for a whole week, and never forgot poor little Tom. And soon My Lady put a pretty little tombstone over Tom's shell in the little churchyard in Vendale, where the old dalesmen all sleep side by side between the limestone crags. And the dame decked it with garlands every Sunday, till she grew so old that she could not stir abroad; then the little children decked it for her.

And always she sang an old old song, as she sat spinning what she called her wedding-dress. The children could not understand it, but they liked it none the less for that; for it was very sweet, and very sad; and that was enough for them. And these are the words of it:

"Where all the world is young, lad,
    And all the trees are green;
And every goose a swan, lad,
    And every lass a queen;
Then hey for boot and horse, lad,
    And round the world away:
Young blood must have its course, lad,
    And every dog his day.

"When all the world is old, lad,
    And all the trees are brown;
And all the sport is stale, lad,
    And all the wheels run down;
Creep home, and take your place there,
    The spent and maimed among:
God grant you find one face there,
    You loved when all was young."

Those are the words: but they are only the body of it: the soul of the song was the dear old woman's sweet face, and sweet voice, and the sweet old air to which she sang; and that, alas! one cannot put on paper. And at last she grew so stiff and lame, that the angels were forced to carry her; and they helped her on with her wedding-dress, and carried her up over Harthover Fells, and a long way beyond that too; and there was a new school-mistress in Vendale.

And all the while Tom was swimming about in the river, with a pretty little lace-collar of gills about his neck, as lively as a grig, and as clean as a fresh-run salmon.

CHAPTER III

CHAPTER III

Tom was now quite amphibious—this means that he could live on land and in water. And he was clean.

For the first time in his life, he felt how comfortable it was to have nothing on him but himself. But he only enjoyed it: he did not know it, or think about it; just as you enjoy life and health, and yet never think about being alive and healthy.

He did not remember having ever been dirty. Indeed, he did not remember any of his old troubles, being tired, or hungry, or beaten, or sent up dark chimneys. Since that sweet sleep, he had forgotten all about his master, and Harthover Place, and the little white girl, and in a word, all that had happened to him when he lived before; and what was best of all, he had forgotten all the bad words which he had learnt from Grimes, and the rude boys with whom he used to play.

And Tom was very happy in the water. He had been sadly overworked in the land-world; and so now, to make up for that, he had nothing but holidays in the water-world for a long, long time to come. He had nothing to do now but enjoy himself, and look at all the pretty things which are to be seen in the cool clear water-world, where the sun is never too hot, and the frost is never too cold.

And what did he live on? Water-cresses, perhaps; or perhaps water-gruel, and water-milk.

Sometimes he went along the smooth gravel waterways, looking at the crickets which ran in and out among the stones, as rabbits do on land; or he climbed over the ledges of rock, and saw the sand-pipes hanging in thousands, with every one of them a pretty little head and legs peeping out; or he went into a still corner, and watched the caddises eating dead sticks, and building their houses with silk and glue. Very fanciful ladies they were; none of them would keep to the same materials for a day. One would begin with some pebbles; then she would stick on a piece of green weed; then she found a shell, and stuck it on too; and the poor shell was alive, and did not like at all being taken to build houses with: but the caddis did not let him have any voice in the matter, being rude and selfish, as vain people are apt to be; then she stuck on a piece of rotten wood, then a very smart pink stone, and so on, till she was patched all over like an Irishman's coat. Then she found a long straw, five times as long as herself, and said, "Hurrah! my sister has a tail, and I'll have one too"; and she stuck it on her back, and marched about with it quite proud, though it was very inconvenient indeed. And, at that, tails became all the fashion among the caddis-baits in that pool, and they all toddled about with long straws sticking out behind, getting between each other's legs, and tumbling over each other, and looking so ridiculous, that Tom laughed at them till he cried.

Then sometimes he came to a deep still reach; and there he saw the water-forests. They would have looked to you only little weeds; but Tom, you must remember, was so little that everything looked a hundred times as big to him as it does to you, just

as things do to a minnow, who sees and catches the little water-creatures which you can only see in a microscope.

And in the water-forest he saw the water-monkeys and water-squirrels (they had all six legs, though; everything almost has six legs in the water, except efts and water-babies); and nimbly enough they ran among the branches. There were water-flowers there, too, in thousands; and Tom tried to pick them: but as soon as he touched them, they drew themselves in and turned into knots of jelly; and then Tom saw that they were all alive—bells, and stars, and wheels, and flowers, of all beautiful shapes and colours; and all alive and busy, just as Tom was. So now he found that there was a great deal more in the world than he had fancied at first sight.

There was one wonderful little fellow, too, who peeped out of the top of a house built of round bricks. He had two big wheels, and one little one, all over teeth, spinning round and round like the wheels in a thrashing-machine; and Tom stood and stared at him, to see what he was going to make with his machinery. And what do you think he was doing? Brick-making. With his two big wheels he swept together all the mud which floated in the water: all that was nice in it he put into his stomach and ate; and all the mud he put into the little wheel on his breast, which really was a round hole set with teeth; and there he spun it into a neat hard round brick; and then he took it and stuck it on the top of his house-wall, and set to work to make another. Now was not he a clever little fellow?

Tom thought so: but when he wanted to talk to him, the

brick-maker was much too busy and proud of his work to take notice of him.

Now you must know that all the things under the water talk: only not such a language as ours; but such as horses, and dogs, and cows, and birds talk to each other; and Tom soon learned to understand them and talk to them; so that he might have had very pleasant company if he had only been a good boy. But I am sorry to say, he was too like some other little boys, very fond of hunting and tormenting creatures for mere sport. Some people say that boys cannot help it; that it is nature, and only a proof that we are all originally descended from beasts of prey. But whether it is nature or not, little boys can help it, and must help it. For if they have naughty, low, mischievous tricks in their nature, as monkeys have, that is no reason why they should give way to those tricks like monkeys, who know no better. And therefore they must not torment dumb creatures; for if they do, a certain old lady who is coming will surely give them exactly what they deserve.

But Tom did not know that; and he pecked and howked the poor water things about sadly, till they were all afraid of him, and got out of his way, or crept into their shells; so he had no one to speak to or play with.

The water-fairies, of course, were very sorry to see him so unhappy, and longed to take him, and tell him how naughty he was, and teach him to be good, and to play and romp with him too: but they had been forbidden to do that. Tom had to learn his lesson for himself by sound and sharp experience.

At last one day he found a caddis, and wanted it to peep out of its house: but its house-door was shut. He had never seen a caddis with a house-door before: so what must he do, the meddle-some little fellow, but pull it open, to see what the poor lady was doing inside. So Tom broke the door, which was the prettiest little grating of silk, stuck all over with shining bits of crystal; and when he looked in, the caddis poked out her head, and it had turned into just the shape of a bird's. But when Tom spoke to her she could not answer; for her mouth and face were tight tied up in a new nightcap of neat pink skin. However, if she didn't answer, all the other caddises did; for they held up their hands and shrieked like the cats in Struwwelpeter: "Oh, you nasty, horrid boy; there you are at it again! And she had just laid herself up for a fortnight's sleep, and then she would have come out with such beautiful wings, and flown about, and laid such lots of eggs: and now you have broken her door, and she can't mend it because her mouth is tied up for a fortnight, and she will die. Who sent you here to worry us out of our lives?"

So Tom swam away. He was very much ashamed of himself, and felt all the naughtier; as little boys do when they have done wrong, and won't say so.

Then he came to a pool full of little trout, and began torment-ing them, and trying to catch them: but they slipped through his fingers, and jumped clean out of water in their fright. But as Tom chased them, he came close to a great dark hover under an alder root, and out floushed a huge old brown trout ten times as big as he was, and ran right against him, and knocked all the breath out of his body; and I don't know which was the more frightened of the two.

Then he went on sulky and lonely, as he deserved to be; and under a bank he saw a very ugly dirty creature sitting, about half as big as himself; which had six legs, and a big stomach, and a most ridiculous head with two great eyes and a face just like a donkey's.

"Oh," said Tom, "you are an ugly fellow to be sure!" and he began making faces at him; and put his nose close to him, and halloed at him, like a very rude boy.

When, hey presto! all the thing's donkey-face came off in a moment, and out popped a long arm with a pair of pincers at the end of it, and caught Tom by the nose. It did not hurt him much; but it held him quite tight.

"Yah, ah! Oh, let me go!" cried Tom.

"Then let me go," said the creature. "I want to be quiet. I want to split."

Tom promised to let him alone, and he let go. "Why do you want to split?" said Tom.

"Because my brothers and sisters have all split, and turned into beautiful creatures with wings; and I want to split too. Don't speak to me. I am sure I shall split. I will split!"

Tom stood still, and watched him. And he swelled himself, and puffed, and stretched himself out stiff, and at last—crack, puff, bang—he opened all down his back, and then up to the top of his head.

And out of his inside came the most slender, elegant, soft creature, as soft and smooth as Tom: but very pale and weak, like a

little child who has been ill a long time in a dark room. It moved
its legs very feebly; and looked about it half ashamed, and then it
began walking slowly up a grass stem to the top of the water.

Tom was so astonished that he never said a word: but he stared
with all his eyes. And he went up to the top of the water too, and
peeped out to see what would happen.

And as the creature sat in the warm bright sun, a wonderful
change came over it. It grew strong and firm; the most lovely
colours began to show on its body, blue and yellow and black,
spots and bars and rings; out of its back rose four great wings of
bright brown gauze; and its eyes grew so large that they filled
all its head, and shone like ten thousand diamonds.

"Oh, you beautiful creature!" said Tom; and he put out his
hand to catch it.

But the thing whirled up into the air, and hung poised on its
wings a moment, and then settled down again by Tom quite
fearless.

"No!" it said, "you cannot catch me. I am a dragon-fly now, the king of all the flies; and I shall dance in the sunshine, and hawk over the river, and catch gnats, and have a beautiful wife like myself. I know what I shall do. Hurrah!" And he flew away into the air, and began catching gnats.

"Oh! come back, come back," cried Tom, "you beautiful creature. I have no one to play with, and I am so lonely here. If you will but come back I will never try to catch you."

"I don't care whether you do or not," said the dragon-fly; "for you can't. But when I have had my dinner, and looked a little about this pretty place, I will come back; and have a little chat about all I have seen in my travels. Why, what a huge tree this is! and what huge leaves on it!"

It was only a big dock-weed: but you know the dragon-fly had never seen any but little water-trees: starwort, and milfoil, and water-crowfoot, and such like; so it did look very big to him. Besides, he was very short-sighted, as all dragon-flies are; and never could see a yard before his nose.

The dragon-fly did come back, and chatted away with Tom. He was a little conceited about his fine colours and his large wings; but, you know, he had been a poor dirty ugly creature all his life before; so there were great excuses for him. He was very fond of talking about all the wonderful things he saw in the trees and the meadows; and Tom liked to listen to him, for he had forgotten all about them. So in a little while they became great friends.

And Tom learnt such a lesson that day, that he did not torment creatures for a long time after. And then the caddises grew quite tame, and used to tell him strange stories about the way they built their houses, and changed their skins, and turned at last into winged flies; till Tom began to long to change his skin, and have wings like them some day.

And the trout and he made it up (for trout very soon forget, if they have been frightened and hurt). So Tom used to play with them at hare and hounds, and great fun they had; and he used to try to leap out of the water, head over heels, as they did before a shower came on: but somehow he never could manage it. He liked most, though, to see them rising at the flies, as they sailed round and round under the shadow of the great oak, where the beetles fell flop into the water, and the green caterpillars let themselves down from the boughs by silk ropes for no reason at all; and then changed their foolish minds for no reason at all either; and hauled themselves up again into the tree, rolling up the rope in a ball between their paws.

And very often Tom caught them just as they touched the water; and caught the alder flies, and the caperers, and the cock-tailed duns and spinners, yellow, and brown, and claret, and grey, and gave them to his friends the trout. Perhaps he was not quite kind to the flies; but one must do a good turn to one's friends when one can.

And at last he gave up catching even the flies; for he made acquaintance with one by accident, and found him a very merry little fellow. And this was the way it happened; and it is all quite true.

He was basking at the top of the water one hot day in July, catching duns and feeding the trout, when he saw a new sort, a dark grey little fellow with a brown head. He was a very little fellow indeed: but he made the most of himself, as people ought to do. He cocked up his head, and he cocked up his wings, and he cocked up his tail, and he cocked up the two whisks at his tail-end, and, in short, he looked the cockiest little man of all little men. And so he proved to be; for instead of getting away, he hopped upon Tom's finger, and sat there as bold as nine tailors; and he cried out in the tiniest, shrillest, squeakiest little voice you ever heard:

"Much obliged to you, indeed; but I don't want it yet."

"Want what?" said Tom, quite taken aback by his impudence.

"Your leg, which you are kind enough to hold out for me to sit on. I must just go and see after my wife for a few minutes. Dear me! what a troublesome business a family is!" (though the idle little rogue did nothing at all, but left his poor wife to lay all the eggs by herself). "When I come back, I shall be glad of it, if you'll be so good as to keep it sticking out just so;" and off he flew.

Tom thought him a very cool sort of personage; and still more so, when in five minutes he came back, and said—"Ah, you were tired waiting? Well, your other leg will do as well."

And he popped himself down on Tom's knee, and began chatting away in his squeaking voice.

"So you live under the water? It's a low place. I lived there for some time; and was very shabby and dirty. But I didn't choose that that should last. So I turned respectable, and came up to the top, and put on this grey suit. It's a very business-like suit, you think, don't you?"

"Very neat and quiet indeed," said Tom.

"Yes, one must be quiet, and neat, and respectable, and all that sort of thing for a little, when one becomes a family man. But I'm tired of it, that's the truth. I've done quite enough business, I consider, in the last week, to last me my life. So I shall put on a ball-dress, and go out and be a smart man, and see the gay world, and have a dance or two. Why shouldn't one be jolly if one can?"

"And what will become of your wife?"

"Oh! she is a very plain stupid creature, and that's the truth; and thinks about nothing but eggs. If she chooses to come, why, she may; and if not, why, I go without her;—and here I go."

And, as he spoke, he turned quite pale, and then quite white.

"Why, you're ill!" said Tom. But he did not answer.

"You're dead," said Tom, looking at him as he stood on his knee as white as a ghost.

"No, I ain't!" answered a little squeaking voice over his head. "This is me up here, in my ball-dress: and that's my skin. Ha, ha! you could not do such a trick as that!"

And no more Tom could, nor all the conjurors in the world. For the little rogue had jumped clean out of his own skin, and left it standing on Tom's knee, eyes, wings, legs, tail, exactly as if it had been alive.

"Ha, ha!" he said, and he jerked and skipped up and down, never stopping an instant, just as if he had St. Vitus's dance. "Ain't I a pretty fellow now?"

And so he was; for his body was white, and his tail orange, and his eyes all the colours of a peacock's tail. And what was the oddest of all, the whisks at the end of his tail had grown five times as long as they were before.

"Ah!" said he, "now I will see the gay world. My living won't cost me much, for I have no mouth, you see, and no inside; so I can never be hungry, nor have the stomach-ache neither."

No more he had. He had grown as dry and hard and empty as a quill, as such silly shallow-hearted fellows deserve to grow.

And he danced up and down for three days and three nights, till he grew so tired, that he tumbled into the water, and floated down. But what became of him Tom never knew.

One day Tom had a new adventure. He was sitting on a water-lily leaf, he and his friend the dragon-fly, watching the gnats dance. The dragon-fly had eaten as many as he wanted, and was sitting quite still and sleepy, for it was very hot and bright. The gnats danced a foot over his head quite happily, and a large black fly settled within an inch of his nose, and began washing his own face and combing his hair with his paws: but the dragon-fly never stirred, and kept on chatting to Tom about the times when he lived under the water.

Suddenly, Tom heard the strangest noise up the stream; cooing, and grunting, and whinning, and squeaking, as if you had put into a bag two stock-doves, nine mice, three guinea-pigs, and a blind puppy, and left them there to settle themselves and make music.

He looked up the water, and there he saw a sight as strange as the noise; a great ball rolling over and over down the stream, seeming one moment of soft brown fur, and the next of shining glass: and yet it was not a ball; for sometimes it broke up and streamed away in pieces, and then it joined again; and all the while the noise came out of it louder and louder.

Tom asked the dragon-fly what it could be: but, of course, with his short sight, he could not even see it, though it was not ten yards away. So he took the neatest little header into the water, and started off to see for himself; and, when he came near, the ball turned out to be four or five beautiful creatures, many times larger than Tom, who were swimming about, and rolling, and diving, and twisting, and wrestling, and cuddling, and kissing, and biting, and scratching, in the most charming fashion that ever was seen. They were young otters and their mother at play.

But, when the biggest of them saw Tom, she darted out from the rest, and cried in the water-language sharply enough, "Quick, children, here is something to eat, indeed!" and came at poor Tom, showing such a wicked pair of eyes, and such a set of sharp teeth in a grinning mouth, that Tom, who had thought her very handsome, said to himself, Handsome is that handsome does, and slipped in between the water-lily roots as fast as he could, and then turned round and made faces at her.

"Come out," said the wicked old otter, "or it will be worse for you."

But Tom looked at her from between two thick roots, and shook them with all his might, making horrible faces all the while, just as he used to grin through the railings at the old women, when he lived before. It was not quite well-bred, no doubt; but you know, Tom had not finished his education yet.

"Come away, children," said the otter in disgust, "it is not worth eating, after all. It is only a nasty eft, which nothing eats, not even those vulgar pike in the pond."

"I am not an eft!" said Tom; "efts have tails."

"You are an eft," said the otter, very positively; "I see your two hands quite plain, and I know you have a tail."

"I tell you I have not," said Tom. "Look here!" and he turned his pretty little self quite round; and, sure enough, he had no more tail than you.

The otter might have got out of it by saying that Tom was a frog: but, like a great many other people, when she had once said a thing, she stood to it, right or wrong; so she answered:

"I say you are an eft, and therefore you are, and not fit for gentlefolk like me and my children. You may stay there till the salmon eat you" (she knew the salmon would not, but she wanted to frighten poor Tom). "Ha! ha! they will eat you, and we will eat them;" and the otter laughed such a wicked cruel laugh—as you may hear them do sometimes; and the first time that you hear it you will probably think it is bogies.

"What are salmon?" asked Tom.

"Fish, you eft, great fish, nice fish to eat. They are the lords of the fish, and we are the lords of the salmon;" and she laughed again. "We hunt them up and down the pools, and drive them up into a corner, the silly things; they are so proud, and bully the little trout, and the minnows, till they see us coming, and then they are so meek all at once; and we catch them, but we disdain to eat them all; we just bite out their soft throats and suck their sweet juice—Oh, so good!"—(and she licked her wicked lips)— "and then throw them away, and go and catch another. They are coming soon, children, coming soon; I can smell the rain coming up off the sea, and then hurrah for a fresh, and salmon, and plenty of eating all day long."

And the otter grew so proud that she turned head over heels twice, and then stood upright half out of the water, grinning like a Cheshire cat.

"And where do they come from?" asked Tom, who kept himself very close, for he was considerably frightened.

"Out of the sea, eft, the great wide sea, where they might stay and be safe if they liked. But out of the sea the silly things come, into the great river down below, and we come up to watch for them; and when they go down again we go down and follow them. And there we fish for the bass and the pollock, and have jolly days along the shore, and toss and roll in the breakers, and sleep snug in the warm dry crags. Ah, that is a merry life too, children, if it were not for those horrid men."

"What are men?" asked Tom; but somehow he seemed to know before he asked.

"Two-legged things, eft: and, now I come to look at you, they are actually something like you, if you had not a tail" (she was determined that Tom should have a tail), "only a great deal bigger, worse luck for us; and they catch the fish with hooks and lines, which get into our feet sometimes, and set pots along the rocks to catch lobsters. They speared my poor dear husband as he went out to find something for me to eat. I was laid up among the crags then, and we were very low in the world, for the sea was so rough that no fish would come in shore. But they speared him, poor fellow, and I saw them carrying him away upon a pole. Ah, he lost his life for your sakes, my children, poor dear obedient creature that he was."

And the otter grew so sentimental (for otters can be very sentimental when they choose, like a good many people who are both cruel and greedy, and no good to anybody at all) that she sailed solemnly away down the burn, and Tom saw her no more for that time. And lucky it was for her that she did so; for no sooner was she gone, than down the bank came seven little rough terrier dogs, snuffing and yapping, and grubbing and splashing, in full cry after the otter. Tom hid among the water-lilies till they were gone; for he could not guess that they were the water-fairies come to help him.

But he could not help thinking of what the otter had said about the great river and the broad sea. And, as he thought, he longed to go and see them. He could not tell why; but the more he thought, the more he grew discontented with the narrow little stream in which he lived, and all his companions there; and wanted to get out into the wide wide world, and enjoy all the wonderful sights of which he was sure it was full.

And once he set off to go down the stream. But the stream was very low; and when he came to the shallows he could not keep under water, for there was no water left to keep under. So the sun burnt his back and made him sick; and he went back again and lay quiet in the pool for a whole week more.

And then, on the evening of a very hot day, he saw a sight.

He had been very stupid all day, and so had the trout; for they would not move an inch to take a fly, though there were thousands on the water, but lay dozing at the bottom under the shade of the stones; and Tom lay dozing too, and was glad to cuddle their smooth cool sides, for the water was quite warm and unpleasant.

But toward evening it grew suddenly dark, and Tom looked up and saw a blanket of black clouds lying right across the valley above his head, resting on the crags right and left. He felt not quite frightened, but very still; for everything was still. There was not a whisper of wind, nor a chirp of a bird to be heard; and next a few great drops of rain fell plop into the water, and one hit Tom on the nose and made him pop his head down quickly enough.

And then the thunder roared, and the lightning flashed, and leaped across Vendale and back again, from cloud to cloud, and cliff to cliff, till the very rocks in the stream seemed to shake; and Tom looked up at it through the water, and thought it the finest thing he ever saw in his life.

But out of the water he dared not put his head; for the rain came down by bucketsful, and the hail hammered like shot on the stream, and churned it into foam; and soon the stream rose, and rushed down, higher and higher, and fouler and fouler, full of beetles, and sticks, and straws, and worms, and addle-eggs, and wood-lice, and leeches, and odds and ends, and omniumgatherums, and this, that, and the other, enough to fill nine museums.

Tom could hardly stand against the stream, and hid behind a

rock. But the trout did not; for out they rushed from among the stones, and began gobbling the beetles and leeches in the most greedy and quarrelsome way, and swimming about with great worms hanging out of their mouths, tugging and kicking to get them away from each other.

And now, by the flashes of the lightning, Tom saw a new sight —all the bottom of the stream alive with great eels, turning and twisting along, all down stream and away. They had been hiding for weeks past in the cracks of the rocks, and in burrows in the mud; and Tom had hardly ever seen them, except now and then at night: but now they were all out, and went hurrying past him so fiercely and wildly that he was quite frightened. And as they hurried past he could hear them say to each other, "We must run, we must run. What a jolly thunderstorm! Down to the sea, down to the sea!"

And then the otter came by with all her brood, twining and sweeping along as fast as the eels themselves; and she spied Tom as she came by, and said:

"Now is your time, eft, if you want to see the world. Come along, children, never mind those nasty eels: we shall breakfast on salmon to-morrow. Down to the sea, down to the sea!"

Then came a flash brighter than all the rest, and by the light of it—in the thousandth part of a second they were gone again—but he had seen them, he was certain of it—Three beautiful little white girls, with their arms twined round each other's necks, floating down the torrent, as they sang, "Down to the sea, down to the sea!"

"Oh stay! Wait for me!" cried Tom; but they were gone: yet he could hear their voices clear and sweet through the roar of thunder and water and wind, singing as they died away, "Down to the sea!"

"Down to the sea?" said Tom; "everything is going to the sea, and I will go too. Good-bye, trout." But the trout were so busy gobbling worms that they never turned to answer him; so that Tom was spared the pain of bidding them farewell.

And now, down the rushing stream, guided by the bright flashes of the storm; past tall birch-fringed rocks, which shone out one moment as clear as day, and the next were dark as night; past dark hovers under swirling banks, from which great trout rushed out on Tom, thinking him to be good to eat, and turned back sulkily, for the fairies sent them home again with a tremendous scolding, for daring to meddle with a water-baby; on through narrow strids and roaring cataracts, where Tom was deafened and blinded for a moment by the rushing waters; along deep reaches, where the white water-lilies tossed and flapped beneath the wind and hail; past sleeping villages; under dark bridge-arches, and away and away to the sea. And Tom could not stop, and did not care to stop; he would see the great world below, and the salmon, and the breakers, and the wide, wide sea.

And when the daylight came, Tom found himself out in the salmon-river.

A full hundred yards broad it was, sliding on from broad pool to broad shallow, and broad shallow to broad pool, over great fields of shingle, under oak and ash coverts, past low cliffs of sandstone, past green meadows, and fair parks, and a great house of grey stone, and brown moors above, and here and there against the sky the smoking chimney of a colliery.

But Tom thought nothing about what the river was like. All his fancy was, to get down to the wide wide sea.

And after a while he came to a place where the river spread out into broad still shallow reaches, so wide that little Tom, as he put his head out of the water, could hardly see across.

And there he stopped. He got a little frightened. "This must be the sea," he thought. "What a wide place it is. If I go on into it I shall surely lose my way, or some strange thing will bite me. I will stop here and look out for the otter, or the eels, or some one to tell me where I shall go."

So he went back a little way, and crept into a crack of the rock, just where the river opened out into the wide shallows, and watched for some one to tell him his way: but the otter and the eels were gone on miles and miles down the stream.

There he waited, and slept too, for he was quite tired with his night's journey; and, when he woke, the stream was clearing to a beautiful amber hue, though it was still very high. And after a while he saw a sight which made him jump up; for he knew in a moment it was one of the things which he had come to look for.

Such a fish! ten times as big as the biggest trout, and a hundred times as big as Tom, sculling up the stream past him, as easily as Tom had sculled down.

Such a fish! shining silver from head to tail, and here and there a crimson dot; with a grand hooked nose, and grand curling lip, and a grand bright eye, looking round him as proudly as a king, and surveying the water right and left as if it all belonged to him. Surely he must be the salmon, the king of all the fish.

Tom was so frightened that he longed to creep into a hole; but he need not have been; for salmon are all true gentlemen, and, like true gentlemen, they look noble and proud enough, and yet, like true gentlemen, they never harm or quarrel with any one, but go about their own business, and leave rude fellows to themselves.

The salmon looked him full in the face, and then went on without minding him, with a swish or two of his tail which made the stream boil again. And in a few minutes came another, and then four or five, and so on; and all passed Tom, rushing and plunging up the cataract with strong strokes of their silver tails, now and then leaping clean out of water and up over a rock, shining gloriously for a moment in the bright sun; while Tom was so delighted that he could have watched them all day long.

And at last one came up bigger than all the rest; but he came slowly, and stopped, and looked back, and seemed very anxious and busy. And Tom saw that he was helping another salmon, an especially handsome one, who had not a single spot upon it, but was clothed in pure silver from nose to tail.

"My dear," said the great fish to his companion, "you really look dreadfully tired, and you must not over-exert yourself at first. Do rest yourself behind this rock;" and he shoved her gently with his nose, to the rock where Tom sat.

You must know that this was the salmon's wife. For salmon,

like other true gentlemen, always choose their lady, and love her, and are true to her, and take care of her, and work for her, and fight for her, as every true gentleman ought; and are not like vulgar chub and roach and pike, who have no high feelings, and take no care of their wives.

Then he saw Tom, and looked at him very fiercely one moment, as if he was going to bite him.

"What do you want here?" he said, very fiercely.

"Oh, don't hurt me!" cried Tom. "I only want to look at you; you are so handsome."

"Ah?" said the salmon, very stately but very civilly. "I really beg your pardon; I see what you are, my little dear. I have met one or two creatures like you before, and found them very agreeable and well-behaved. Indeed, one of them showed me a great kindness lately, which I hope to be able to repay. I hope we shall not be in your way here. As soon as this lady is rested, we shall proceed on our journey."

What a well-bred old salmon he was!

"So you have seen things like me before?" asked Tom.

"Several times, my dear. Indeed, it was only last night that one at the river's mouth came and warned me and my wife of some new stake-nets which had got into the stream, I cannot tell how, since last winter, and showed us the way round them in the most charmingly obliging way."

"So there are babies in the sea?" cried Tom, and clapped his little hands. "Then I shall have some one to play with there? How delightful!"

"Were there no babies up this stream?" asked the lady salmon.

"No; and I grew so lonely. I thought I saw three last night: but they were gone in an instant, down to the sea. So I went too; for I had nothing to play with but caddises and dragon-flies and trout."

"Ugh!" cried the lady, "what low company!"

"My dear, if he has been in low company, he has certainly not learnt their low manners," said the salmon.

"No, indeed, poor little dear: but how sad for him to live among such people as caddises, who have actually six legs, the nasty things; and dragon-flies, too! why they are not even good to eat; for I tried them once, and they are all hard and empty; and, as for trout, every one knows what they are." Whereon she curled up her lip, and looked dreadfully scornful, while her husband curled up his too, till he looked as proud as Alcibiades.

"Why do you dislike the trout so?" asked Tom.

"My dear, we do not even mention them, if we can help it; for I am sorry to say they are relations of ours who do us no credit. A great many years ago they were just like us; but they were so lazy, and cowardly, and greedy, that instead of going down to the sea every year to see the world and grow strong and fat, they chose to stay and poke about in the little streams and eat worms and grubs: and they are very properly punished for it; for they have grown ugly and brown and spotted and small; and are actually so degraded in their tastes, that they will eat our children."

"And then they pretend to scrape acquaintance with us again," said the lady. "Why, I have actually known one of them propose to a lady salmon, the impudent little creature."

"I should hope," said the gentleman, "that there are very few ladies of our race who would degrade themselves by listening to such a creature for an instant. If I saw such a thing happen, I should consider it my duty to put them both to death upon the spot." So the old salmon said, like an old blue-blooded hidalgo of Spain: and what is more, he would have done it too. For you must know, no enemies are so bitter against each other as those who are of the same race; and a salmon looks on a trout as something just too much like himself to be tolerated.

CHAPTER IV

CHAPTER IV

So the salmon went up, after Tom had warned them of the wicked old otter; and Tom went down, but slowly and cautiously, coasting along the shore. He was many days about it, for it was many miles down to the sea; and perhaps he would never have found his way, if the fairies had not guided him, without his seeing their fair faces, or feeling their gentle hands.

And, as he went, he had a very strange adventure. It was a clear still September night, and the moon shone so brightly down through the water, that he could not sleep, though he shut his eyes as tight as possible. So at last he came up to the top, and sat upon a little point of rock, and looked up at the broad yellow moon, and wondered what she was, and thought that she looked at him. And he watched the moonlight on the rippling river, and the black heads of the firs, and the silver-frosted lawns, and listened to the owl's hoot, and the snipe's bleat, and the fox's bark, and the otter's laugh; and smelt the soft perfume of the birches, and the wafts of heather honey off the grouse-moor far above; and felt very happy, though he could not well tell why. You, of course, would have been very cold sitting there on a September night, without the least bit of clothes on your wet back; but Tom was a water-baby, and therefore felt cold no more than a fish.

Suddenly, he saw a beautiful sight. A bright red light moved along the river side, and threw down into the water a long tap-root of flame. Tom, curious little rogue that he was, must needs go and see what it was; so he swam to the shore, and met the light as it stopped over a shallow run at the edge of a low rock.

And there, underneath the light, lay five or six great salmon, looking up at the flame with their great goggle eyes, and wagging their tails, as if they were very much pleased at it.

Tom came to the top, to look at this wonderful light nearer, and made a splash.

And he heard a voice say:

"There was a fish rose."

He did not know what the words meant: but he seemed to know the sound of them, and to know the voice which spoke them; and he saw on the bank three great two-legged creatures, one of whom held the light, flaring and sputtering, and another a long pole. And he knew that they were men, and was frightened, and crept into a hole in the rock, from which he could see what went on.

The man with the torch bent down over the water, and looked earnestly in; and then he said:

"Tak that muckle fellow, lad; he's ower fifteen pounds; and haud your hand steady."

Tom felt that there was some danger coming, and longed to warn the foolish salmon, who kept staring up at the light as if he was bewitched. But, before he could make up his mind, down came the pole through the water; there was a fearful splash and struggle, and Tom saw that the salmon was speared right through, and was lifted out of the water.

And then, from behind, there sprang on these three men three other men; and there were shouts, and blows, and words which Tom recollected to have heard before; and he shuddered and turned sick at them now, for he felt somehow that they were strange, and ugly, and wrong, and horrible. And it all began to come back to him. They were men; and they were fighting; savage, desperate, up-and-down fighting, such as Tom had seen too many times before.

And he stopped his little ears, and longed to swim away; and was very glad that he was a water-baby, and had nothing to do any more with horrid dirty men, with foul clothes on their backs, and foul words on their lips: but he dared not stir out of his hole; while the rock shook over his head with the trampling and struggling of the keepers and the poachers.

All of a sudden there was a tremendous splash, and a frightful flash, and a hissing, and all was still.

For into the water, close to Tom, fell one of the men; he who held the light in his hand. Into the swift river he sank, and rolled over and over in the current. Tom heard the men above run along, seemingly looking for him: but he drifted down into the deep hole below, and there lay quite still, and they could not find him.

Tom waited a long time, till all was quiet; and then he peeped out, and saw the man lying. At last he screwed up his courage, and swam down to him. "Perhaps," he thought, "the water has made him fall asleep, as it did me."

Then he went nearer. He grew more and more curious, he could not tell why. He must go and look at him. He would go very quietly, of course; so he swam round and round him, closer and closer; and, as he did not stir, at last he came quite close and looked him in the face.

The moon shone so bright that Tom could see every feature; and, as he saw, he recollected, bit by bit. It was his old master, Grimes.

Tom turned tail, and swam away as fast as he could.

"Oh dear me!" he thought, "now he will turn into a water-baby. What a nasty troublesome one he will be! And perhaps he will find me, and beat me again."

So he went up the river again a little way, and lay there the rest of the night under an alder root; but, when morning came, he longed to go down again to the big pool, and see whether Mr. Grimes had turned into a water-baby yet.

So he went very carefully, peeping round all the rocks, and hiding under all the roots. Mr. Grimes lay there still; he had not turned into a water-baby. In the afternoon Tom went back again. He could not rest till he had found out what had become of Mr. Grimes. But this time Mr. Grimes was gone; and Tom made up his mind that he was turned into a water-baby.

He need not have worried, poor little man; Mr. Grimes did not turn into a water-baby, or anything like one at all. But he did worry; and a long time he was fearful lest he should meet Grimes suddenly in some deep pool. He could not know that the fairies had carried him away, and put him, where they put everything which falls into the water, exactly where it ought to be.

Then Tom went on down the wide river, for he was afraid of staying near Grimes; and as he went, all the vale looked sad. The red and yellow leaves showered down into the river; the flies and beetles were all dead and gone; the chill autumn fog lay low upon the hills, and sometimes spread itself so thickly on the river, that he could not see his way. But he felt his way instead, following the flow of the stream, day after day, past great bridges, past boats

and barges, past the great town, with its wharfs, and mills, and
tall smoking chimneys, and ships which rode at anchor in the
stream; and now and then he ran against their hawsers, and wondered what they were, and peeped out, and saw the sailors lounging
on board, smoking their pipes; and ducked under again, for he was
terribly afraid of being caught by man and turned into a chimney-
sweep once more. He did not know that the fairies were close to
him always, shutting the sailors' eyes lest they should see him, and
turning him aside from millraces, and sewer-mouths, and all foul
and dangerous things. Poor little fellow, it was a dreary journey for
him; and more than once he longed to be back in Vendale, playing
with the trout in the bright summer sun. But it could not be.
What has been once can never come over again. And people can
be little babies, even water-babies, only once in their lives.

Besides, people who make up their minds to go and see the
world, as Tom did, must needs find it a weary journey. Lucky for
them if they do not lose heart and stop half-way, instead of going
on bravely to the end as Tom did. For then they will remain
neither boys nor men, neither fish, flesh, nor good red herring;
having learnt a great deal too much, and yet not enough; and
sown their wild oats, without having the advantage of reaping
them.

But Tom was always a brave, determined little boy who never
knew when he was beaten; and on and on he held, till he saw, a
long way off, the red buoy through the fog. And then he found, to
his surprise, the stream turned round, and running up inland.

It was the tide, of course; but Tom knew nothing of the tide.

He only knew that in a minute more the water, which had been fresh, turned salt all round him. And then there came a change over him. He felt as strong, and light, and fresh as if his veins had run champagne; and gave, he did not know why, three skips out of the water, a yard high, and head over heels, just as the salmon do when they first touch the noble rich salt water, which, as some wise men tell us, is the mother of all living things.

He did not care now for the tide being against him. The red buoy was in sight, dancing in the open sea; and to the buoy he would go, and to it he went. He passed great shoals of bass and mullet, leaping and rushing in after the shrimps, but he never heeded them, or they him; and once he passed a great black shining seal, who was coming in after the mullet. The seal put his head and shoulders out of water, and stared at him, looking exactly like a fat and wrinkled old man with a grey pate. And Tom, instead of being frightened, said, "How d'ye do, sir; what a beautiful place the sea is!" And the old seal, instead of trying to bite him, looked at him with his soft sleepy winking eyes, and said, "Good tide to you, my little man; are you looking for your brothers and sisters? I passed them all at play outside."

"Oh, then," said Tom, "I shall have playfellows at last!" and he swam on to the buoy, and got upon it (for he was quite out of breath) and sat there, and looked round for water-babies: but there were none to be seen.

The sea-breeze came in freshly with the tide, and blew the fog away; and the little waves danced for joy around the buoy, and the old buoy danced with them. The shadows of the clouds ran races over the bright blue bay, and yet never caught each other up: and the breakers plunged merrily upon the wide white sands, and jumped up over the rocks, to see what the green fields inside were like, and tumbled down and broke themselves all to pieces, and never minded it a bit, but mended themselves and jumped up again. And the terns hovered over Tom like huge white dragon-flies with black heads, and the gulls laughed like girls at play, and the sea-pies, with their red bills and legs, flew to and fro from shore to shore, and whistled sweet and wild. And Tom looked and looked, and listened; and he would have been very happy, if he could only have seen the water-babies. Then, when the tide turned, he left the buoy, and swam round and round in search of them: but in vain. Sometimes he thought he heard them laughing: but it was only the laughter of the ripples. And sometimes he thought he saw them at the bottom: but it was only white and pink shells. And once he was sure he had found one, for he saw two bright eyes peeping out of the sand. So he dived down, and began scraping the sand away, and cried, "Don't hide; I do want some one to play with so much!" And out jumped a great turbot, with his ugly eyes and mouth all awry, and flopped away along the bottom, knocking poor Tom over. And he sat down at the bottom of the sea, and cried salt tears from sheer disappointment.

To have come all this way, and faced so many dangers, and yet to find no water-babies! How hard!

And Tom sat upon the buoy long days, long weeks, looking out to sea, and wondering when the water-babies would come back; and yet they never came.

Then he began to ask all the strange things which came in out of the sea if they had seen any; and some said "Yes," and some said nothing at all.

He asked the bass and the pollock; but they were so greedy after the shrimps that they did not care to answer him a word.

Then there came in a whole fleet of purple sea-snails, floating along each on a sponge full of foam, and Tom said, "Where do you come from, you pretty creatures? And have you seen the water-babies?"

And the sea-snails answered, "Whence we come we know not;

and whither we are going, who can tell? We float out our little
life in the mid-ocean, with the warm sunshine above our heads,
and the warm gulf-stream below; and that is enough for us. Yes,
perhaps we have seen the water-babies. We have seen many
strange things as we sailed along." And they floated away, the
happy stupid things, and all went ashore upon the sands.

Then there came in a great lazy sunfish, as big as a fat pig cut in
half; and he seemed to have been cut in half too, and squeezed in
a clothes-press till he was flat; but to all his big body and big fins he
had only a little rabbit's mouth, no bigger than Tom's; and, when
Tom questioned him, he answered in a little squeaky feeble voice:

"I'm sure I don't know, I've lost my way. I meant to go to the
Chesapeake, and I'm afraid I've got wrong, somehow. Dear me!
it was all by following that pleasant warm water. I'm sure I've lost
my way."

And, when Tom asked him again, he could only answer, "I've
lost my way. Don't talk to me, I want to think."

Then there came by a shoal of porpoises, rolling as they
went—papas, and mammas, and little children—and all quite
smooth and shiny, because the fairies French-polish them every
morning; and they sighed so softly as they came by, that
Tom took courage to speak to them: but all they answered

was, "Hush, hush, hush"; for that was all they had learnt to say.

And then there came a shoal of basking sharks, some of them as long as a boat, and Tom was frightened at them. But they were very lazy, good-natured fellows, not greedy tyrants, like white sharks and blue sharks and ground sharks and hammer-heads, who eat men, or saw-fish and threshers and ice-sharks, who hunt the poor old whales. They came and rubbed their great sides against the buoy, and lay basking in the sun with their back fins out of water; and winked at Tom: but he never could get them to speak. They had eaten so many herrings that they were quite stupid; and Tom was glad when a collier brig came by, and frightened them all away; for they did smell most horribly, certainly, and he had to hold his nose tight as long as they were there.

And then there came by a beautiful creature, like a ribbon of pure silver with a sharp head and very long teeth: but it seemed very sick and sad. Sometimes it rolled helpless on its side; and then it dashed away glittering like white fire; and then it lay sick again and motionless.

"Where do you come from?" asked Tom. "And why are you so sick and sad?"

"I come from the warm Carolinas, and the sandbanks fringed with pines; where the great owl-rays leap and flap, like giant bats,

upon the tide. But I wandered north and north, upon the treacher-
ous warm gulf-stream, till I met with the cold icebergs, afloat in
the mid-ocean. So I got tangled among the icebergs, and chilled
with their frozen breath. But the water-babies helped me from
among them, and set me free again. And now I am mending every
day; but I am very sick and sad; and perhaps I shall never get home
again to play with the owl-rays any more."

"Oh!" cried Tom. "And you have seen water-babies? Have
you seen any near here?"

"Yes; they helped me again last night, or I should have been
eaten by a great black porpoise."

How vexatious! The water-babies close to him, and yet he
could not find one.

And then he left the buoy, and used to go along the sands and
round the rocks, and come out in the night and sit upon a point
of rock, among the shining sea-weeds, in the low October tides,
and cry and call for the water-babies: but he never heard a voice
call in return. And, at last, with his fretting and crying, he grew
quite lean and thin.

But one day among the rocks he found a playfellow. It was not
a water-baby, alas! but it was a lobster; and a very distinguished
lobster he was; for he had live barnacles on his claws, which is a
great mark of distinction in lobsterdom, and no more to be
bought for money than a good conscience or the Victoria Cross.

Tom had never seen a lobster before; and he was mightily
taken with this one; for he thought him the most curious, odd,
ridiculous creature he had ever seen; and there he was not far

wrong; for all the ingenious men, and all the scientific men, and all the fanciful men, in the world could never invent, if all their wits were boiled into one, anything so curious, and so ridiculous, as a lobster.

He had one claw knobbed and the other jagged; and Tom delighted in watching him hold on to the sea-weed with his knobbed claw, while he cut up salads with his jagged one, and then put them in his mouth, after smelling at them, like a monkey. And always the little barnacles threw out their casting nets and swept the water, and came in for their share of whatever there was for dinner.

But Tom was most astonished to see how he fired himself off— snap! like the leap-frogs which you make out of a goose's breast-bone. Certainly he took the most wonderful shots, and backwards, too. For, if he wanted to go into a narrow crack ten yards off, what do you think he did? If he had gone in head foremost, of course he could not have turned round. So he used to turn his tail to it, and lay his long horns, which carry his sixth sense in their tips (and nobody knows what that sixth sense is), straight down his back to guide him, and twist his eyes back till they almost came out of their sockets, and then make ready, present, fire, snap!—and away he went, pop into the hole; and peeped out and twiddled his whiskers, as much as to say, "You couldn't do that."

Tom asked him about water-babies. "Yes," he said. He had seen them often. But he did not think much of them. They were meddlesome little creatures, that went about helping fish and shells which got into scrapes. Well, for his part, he should be

ashamed to be helped by little soft creatures that had not even a
shell on their backs. He had lived quite long enough in the world
to take care of himself.

He was a conceited fellow, the old lobster, and not very civil to
Tom; and you will hear how he had to alter his mind before he
was done, as conceited people generally have. But he was so funny,
and Tom so lonely, that he could not quarrel with him; and they
used to sit in holes in the rocks, and chat for hours.

And about this time there happened to Tom a very strange and
important adventure—so important, indeed, that he was very near
never finding the water-babies at all.

I hope that you have not forgotten the little white lady all this
while. For it befell in the pleasant short December days, when
Sir John was so busy hunting that nobody at home could get a

word out of him, that My Lady determined to take all the children to the sea-side for a change of air. And it befell that, on the very shore, and over the very rocks, where Tom was sitting with his friend the lobster, there walked one day the little white lady, Ellie herself, and with her a very wise man indeed—Professor Ptthmllnsprts, which is a very ancient and noble Polish name.

He was, as I said, a very great naturalist, and chief professor of Necrobioneopalæonthydrochthonanthropopithekology in the new university which the king of the Cannibal Islands had founded; and, being a member of the Acclimatisation Society, he had come here to collect all the nasty things which he could find on the coast of England, and turn them loose round the Cannibal Islands, because they had not nasty things enough there to eat what they left.

But he was a very worthy kind good-natured little old gentleman; and very fond of children (for he was not the least a cannibal himself); and very good to all the world as long as it was good to him.

He had met Sir John at Scarborough, or Fleetwood, or somewhere or other, and had made acquaintance with him, and become very fond of his children.

So Ellie and he were walking on the rocks, and he was showing her about one in ten thousand of all the beautiful and curious things which are to be seen there. But little Ellie was not satisfied with them at all. She liked much better to play with live children, or even with dolls, which she could pretend were alive; and at last she said honestly, "I don't care about all these things, because they can't play with me, or talk to me. If there were little children now in the water, as there used to be, and I could see them, I should like that."

"Children in the water, you strange little duck?" said the professor.

"Yes," said Ellie. "I know there used to be children in the water, and mermaids too, and mermen. I saw them all in a picture at home, of a beautiful lady sailing in a car drawn by dolphins, and babies flying round her, and one sitting in her lap; and the mermaids swimming and playing, and the mermen trumpeting on conch-shells; and it is called 'The Triumph of Galatea'; and there is a burning mountain in the picture behind. It hangs on the great staircase, and I have looked at it ever since I was a baby, and dreamed about it a hundred times; and it is so beautiful, that it must be true."

But the professor had not the least notion of allowing that things were true merely because they were beautiful, so he was not inclined to be of little Ellie's opinion. Instead he gave her an outline, in a form suited to her youthful mind, of a paper he had given at the British Association, in which he had said that nymphs, satyrs, dwarfs, trolls, elves, gnomes, fairies, brownies and other sprites, including angels and archangels, goblins, imps and bogies, were nothing at all, and pure bosh and wind.

Now little Ellie was, perhaps, a stupid little girl; for, instead of being convinced by Professor Ptthmllnsprts' arguments, she only asked the same question over again.

"But why are there not water-babies?"

I trust and hope that it was because the professor trod at that moment on the edge of a very sharp mussel, and hurt one of his corns sadly, that he answered quite sharply,

"Because there ain't."

Which was not even good English; the professor ought to have said, if he was so angry as to say anything of the kind—because there are not: or are none: or are none of them: or because they do not exist.

And he groped with his net under the weeds so violently, that, as it befell, he caught poor little Tom.

He felt the net very heavy; and lifted it out quickly, with Tom all entangled in the meshes.

"Dear me!" he cried. "What a large pink Holothurian; with hands, too! It must be connected with Synapta."

And he took him out.

"It has actually eyes!" he cried. "Why, it must be a Cephalopod! This is most extraordinary!"

"No, I ain't!" cried Tom, as loud as he could; for he did not like to be called names.

"It is a water-baby!" cried Ellie; and of course it was.

"Water-fiddlesticks, my dear!" said the professor; and he turned away sharply.

There was no denying it. It was a water-baby: and he had said a moment ago that there were none. What was he to do?

He would have liked, of course, to have taken Tom home in a bucket. He would not have put him in spirits. Of course not. He would have kept him alive, and petted him (for he was a very kind old gentleman), and written a book about him. But—what would all the learned men say to him after his speech at the British Association? And what would Ellie say, after what he had just told her?

Now, if the professor had said to Ellie, "Yes, my darling, it is a water-baby, and a very wonderful thing it is; and it shows how little I know of the wonders of nature, in spite of forty years' honest labour. I was just telling you that there could be no such creatures: and, behold! here is one come to confound my conceit." If the professor had said that, then little Ellie would have believed him more firmly, and respected him more deeply, and loved him better, than ever she had done before. But he was of a different opinion. He hesitated a moment. He longed to keep Tom, and yet he half wished he never had caught him; and, at last, he quite longed to get rid of him. So he turned away, and poked Tom with his finger, for want of anything better to do; and said carelessly, "My dear little maid, you must have dreamed of water-babies last night, your head is so full of them."

Now Tom had been in the most horrible and unspeakable fright all the while; and had kept as quiet as he could, though he was called a Holothurian and a Cephalopod; for it was fixed in his little head that if a man with clothes on caught him, he might put clothes on him too, and make a dirty black chimney-sweep of him again. But when the professor poked him, it was more than he could bear; and, between fright and rage, he turned to bay as valiantly as a mouse in a corner, and bit the professor's finger till it bled.

"Oh! ah! yah!" cried the professor and glad of an excuse to

be rid of Tom, dropped him on to the sea-weed, and thence he
dived into the water, and was gone in a moment.

"But it was a water-baby, and I heard it speak!" cried Ellie.
"Ah, it is gone!" And she jumped down off the rock to try and
catch Tom before he slipped into the sea.

Too late! and what was worse, as she sprang down, she
slipped, and fell some six feet, hit her head on a rock, and lay
quite still.

The professor picked her up, and tried to waken her, and called
to her, and cried over her, for he loved her very much: but she
would not waken at all. So he took her up in his arms, and carried
her to her governess, and they all went home; and little Ellie was
put to bed, and lay there quite still; only now and then she woke
up, and called out about the water-baby: but no one knew what
she meant, and the professor did not tell, for he was ashamed to
tell.

And, after a week, one moonlight night, the fairies came flying in at the window, and brought her such a pretty pair of wings, that she could not help putting them on; and she flew with them out of the window, and over the land, and over the sea, and up through the clouds, and nobody heard or saw anything of her for a very long while.

CHAPTER V

CHAPTER V

But what became of little Tom?

He slipped away off the rocks into the water, as I said before. But he could not help thinking of little Ellie. He did not remember who she was; but he knew that she was a little girl, though she was a hundred times as big as he. This is not surprising: size has nothing to do with kindred. A tiny weed may be first cousin to a great tree.

So Tom knew that Ellie was a little girl, and thought about her all that day, and longed to have her to play with; but he had very soon to think of something else. And here is the account of what happened to him, as it was published next morning in the *Waterproof Gazette*, on the finest watered paper, for the use of the great fairy, Mrs. Bedonebyasyoudid, who reads the news very carefully every morning, and especially the police cases, as you will hear very soon.

He was going along the rocks in three-fathom water, watching the pollock catch prawns, and the wrasses nibble barnacles off the rocks, shells and all, when he saw a round cage of green withes; and inside it, looking very much ashamed of himself, sat his friend the lobster, twiddling his horns, instead of thumbs.

"What, have you been naughty, and have they put you in the lock-up?" asked Tom.

The lobster felt a little indignant at such a notion, but he was too much depressed in spirits to argue; so he only said, "I can't get out."

"Why did you get in?"

"After that nasty piece of dead fish." He had thought it looked and smelt very nice when he was outside, and so it did, for a lobster: but now he turned round and abused it because he was angry with himself.

"Where did you get in?"

"Through that round hole at the top."

"Then why don't you get out through it?"

"Because I can't;" and the lobster twiddled his horns more fiercely than ever, but he was forced to confess:

"I have jumped upwards, downwards, backwards, and side-ways, at least four thousand times; and I can't get out: I always get up underneath there, and can't find the hole."

Tom looked at the trap, and having more wit than the lobster, he saw plainly enough what was the matter; as you may if you will look at a lobster-pot.

"Stop a bit," said Tom. "Turn your tail up to me, and I'll pull you through hindforemost, and then you won't stick in the spikes."

But the lobster was so stupid and clumsy that he couldn't hit the hole.

Tom reached and clawed down the hole after him, till he caught hold of him; and then, as was to be expected, the clumsy lobster pulled him in headforemost.

"Hullo! here is a pretty business," said Tom. "Now take your

great claws, and break the points off those spikes, and then we
shall both get out easily."

"Dear me, I never thought of that," said the lobster; "and
after all the experience of life that I have had!"

You see, experience is of very little good unless a man, or a
lobster, has wit enough to make use of it.

But they had not got half the spikes away, when they saw a
great dark cloud over them; and lo and behold, it was the otter.

How she did grin and grin when she saw Tom. "Yar!" said she, "you little meddlesome wretch, I have you now! I will serve you out for telling the salmon where I was!" And she crawled all over the pot to get in.

Tom was horribly frightened, and still more frightened when she found the hole in the top, and squeezed herself right down through it, all eyes and teeth. But no sooner was her head inside than valiant Mr. Lobster caught her by the nose, and held on.

And there they were all three in the pot, rolling over and over, and very tight packing it was. And the lobster tore at the otter, and the otter tore at the lobster, and both squeezed and thumped poor Tom till he had no breath left in his body; and I don't know what would have happened to him if he had not at last got on the otter's back, and safe out of the hole.

He was right glad when he got out: but he would not desert his friend who had saved him; and the first time he saw his tail uppermost he caught hold of it, and pulled with all his might.

But the lobster would not let go.

"Come along," said Tom; "don't you see she is dead?" And so she was, quite drowned and dead.

And that was the end of the wicked otter.

But the lobster would not let go.

"Come along, you stupid old stick-in-the-mud," cried Tom, "or the fisherman will catch you!" And that was true, for Tom felt some one above beginning to haul up the pot.

But the lobster would not let go.

Tom saw the fisherman haul him up to the boat-side, and

thought it was all up with him. But when Mr. Lobster saw the fisherman, he gave such a furious and tremendous snap, that he snapped out of his hand, and out of the pot, and safe into the sea. But he left his knobbed claw behind him; for it never came into his stupid head to let go after all, so he just shook his claw off as the easier method.

Tom asked the lobster why he never thought of letting go. He said very determinedly that it was a point of honour among lobsters.

And now happened to Tom a most wonderful thing; for he had not left the lobster five minutes before he came upon a water-baby.

A real live water-baby, sitting on the white sand, very busy about a little point of rock. And when it saw Tom it looked up for a moment, and then cried, "Why, you are not one of us. You are a new baby! Oh, how delightful!"

And it ran to Tom, and Tom ran to it, and they hugged and kissed each other for ever so long, they did not know why. But they did not need any introductions there under the water.

At last Tom said, "Oh, where have you been all this while? I have been looking for you so long, and I have been so lonely."

"We have been here for days and days. There are hundreds of us about the rocks. How was it you did not see us, or hear us when we sing and romp every evening before we go home?"

Tom looked at the baby again, and then he said:

"Well, this is wonderful! I have seen things just like you again and again, but I thought you were shells, or sea-creatures. I never took you for water-babies like myself."

Now, was not that very odd? So odd, indeed, that you will, no doubt, want to know how it happened, and why Tom could never find a water-baby till after he had got the lobster out of the pot. And, if you will read this story nine times over, and then think for yourself, you will find out why.

"Now," said the baby, "come and help me, or I shall not have finished before my brothers and sisters come, and it is time to go home."

"What shall I help you at?"

"At this poor dear little rock; a great clumsy boulder came rolling by in the last storm, and knocked all its head off, and rubbed off all its flowers. And now I must plant it again with sea-weeds, and coralline, and anemones, and I will make it the prettiest little rock-garden on all the shore."

So they worked away at the rock, and planted it, and smoothed the sand down round it, and capital fun they had till the tide began to turn. And then Tom heard all the other babies coming, laughing and singing and shouting and romping; and the noise they made was just like the noise of the ripple. So he knew that he had been hearing and seeing the water-babies all along; only he did not know them, because his eyes and ears were not opened.

And in they came, dozens and dozens of them, some bigger than Tom and some smaller, all in the neatest little white bathing dresses; and when they found that he was a new baby they hugged him and kissed him, and then put him in the middle and danced round him on the sand, and there was no one ever so happy as poor little Tom.

"Now then," they all cried at once, "we must come away home, we must come away home, or the tide will leave us dry. We have mended all the broken sea-weed, and put all the rock pools in order, and planted all the shells again in the sand, and nobody will see where the ugly storm swept in last week."

And this is the reason why the rock pools are always so neat and clean; because the water-babies come in shore after every storm, to sweep them out, and comb them down, and put them all to rights again.

And where is the home of the water-babies? In St. Brandan's fairy isle.

Did you never hear of the blessed St. Brandan, how he preached to the wild Irish, on the wild wild Kerry coast; he and five other hermits, till they were weary, and longed to rest? For the wild Irish would not listen to them, and they would not learn to be peaceable Christians at all.

So St. Brandan went out to the point of old Dunmore, and looked over the tide-way roaring round the Blasquets, at the end of all the world, and away into the ocean, and sighed—"Ah that I had wings as a dove!" And far away, before the setting sun, he saw a blue fairy sea, and golden fairy islands, and he said, "Those are the islands of the blest." Then he and his friends got into a hooker, and sailed away and away to the westward, and were never heard of more.

And when St. Brandan and the hermits came to that fairy isle, they found it overgrown with cedars, and full of beautiful birds; and he sat down under the cedars, and preached to all the birds in the air. And they liked his sermons so well that they told the fishes in the sea; and they came, and St. Brandan preached to them; and the fishes told the water-babies, who live in the caves under the Isle; and they came up by hundreds every Sunday, and St. Brandan got quite a neat little Sunday-school. And there he taught the water-babies for a great many hundred years, till his eyes grew too dim to see, and his beard grew so long that he dared not walk for fear of treading on it, and then he might have tumbled down. And at last he and the five hermits fell fast asleep under the cedar shades, and there they sleep unto this day. But the fairies took to the water-babies, and taught them their lessons themselves.

And some say that St. Brandan will awake, and begin to teach the babies once more: but some think that he will sleep on, for better for worse, till the coming of the Cocqcigrues. But, on still clear summer evenings, when the sun sinks down into the sea, among golden cloud-capes and cloud-islands, and locks and friths of azure sky, the sailors fancy that they see, away to westward, St. Brandan's fairy isle.

But whether men can see it or not, St. Brandan's Isle once actually stood there; a great land out in the ocean, which has sunk and sunk beneath the waves. Old Plato called it Atlantis, and told strange tales of the wise men who lived therein, and of the wars they fought in the old times. And from off that island came strange flowers, which linger still about this land:—the Cornish heath, and Cornish moneywort, and the delicate Venus's hair, and the London-pride which covers the Kerry mountains, and the little pink butterwort of Devon and the great blue butterwort of Ireland, and the Connemara heath, and the bristle-fern of the Turk waterfall, and many a strange plant more; all fairy tokens left for wise men and good children from off St. Brandan's Isle.

Now when Tom got there, he found that the isle stood all on pillars, and that its roots were full of caves. There were pillars of black basalt, like Staffa; and pillars of green and crimson serpentine, like Kynance; and pillars ribboned with red and white and yellow sandstone, like Livermead; and there were blue grottoes, like Capri; and white grottoes, like Adelsberg; all curtained and draped with seaweeds, purple and crimson, green and brown; and strewn with soft white sand, on which the water-babies sleep every night. But, to keep the place clean and sweet, the crabs picked up all the scraps off the floor, and ate them like so many monkeys; while the rocks were covered with ten thousand sea-anemones, and corals and madrepores, who scavenged the water all day long, and kept it nice and pure.

And, instead of watchmen and policemen to keep out nasty things at night, there were thousands and thousands of water-snakes, and most wonderful creatures they were. They were all named after the Nereids, the sea fairies who took care of them, Eunice and Polynoe, Phyllodoce and Psamathe, and all the rest of the pretty darlings who swim round their Queen Amphitrite, and her car of cameo shell. They were dressed in green velvet, and black velvet, and purple velvet; and were all jointed in rings; and some of them had three hundred brains apiece, so that they must have been uncommonly shrewd detectives; and some had eyes in their tails; and some had eyes in every joint, so that they kept a very sharp look-out; and when they wanted a baby-snake, they just grew one at the end of their own tails, and when it was able to take care of itself it dropped off; so that they brought up their families very cheaply.

If only Tom had given up all his naughty tricks, and left off tormenting dumb animals, now that he had plenty of playfellows to amuse him. Instead of that, he would meddle with the creatures, all but the water-snakes, for they would stand no nonsense. So he tickled the madrepores, to make them shut up; and frightened the crabs, to make them hide in the sand and peep out at him with the tips of their eyes; and put stones into the anemones' mouths to make them fancy that their dinner was coming.

The other children warned him, and said, "Take care what you are at. Mrs. Bedonebyasyoudid is coming." But Tom never heeded them, being quite riotous with high spirits and good luck, till, one Friday morning early, Mrs. Bedonebyasyoudid came indeed.

A very tremendous lady she was; and when the children saw her, they all stood in a row, very upright indeed, and smoothed down their bathing dresses, and put their hands behind them, just as if they were going to be examined by the inspector.

And she had on a black bonnet, and a black shawl, and no crinoline at all; and a pair of large green spectacles, and a great hooked nose, hooked so much that the bridge of it stood quite up above her eyebrows; and under her arm she carried a great birch-rod. Indeed, she was so ugly, that Tom was tempted to make faces at her: but did not; for he did not admire the look of the birch-rod under her arm.

And she looked at the children one by one, and seemed very much pleased with them, though she never asked them one question about how they were behaving; and then began giving them all sorts of nice sea-things—sea-cakes, sea-apples, sea-oranges, sea-bull's-eyes, sea-toffee; and to the very best of all she gave sea-ices, made out of sea-cow's cream, which never melt under water.

Now little Tom watched all these sweet things given away, till his mouth watered, and his eyes grew as round as an owl's. For he hoped that his turn would come at last; and so it did. For the lady called him up, and held out her fingers with something in them, and popped it into his mouth; and, lo and behold, it was a nasty cold hard pebble.

"You are a very cruel woman," said he, and began to whimper.

"And you are a very cruel boy, who puts pebbles into the sea-anemones' mouths, to tease them and make them fancy that

they had caught a good dinner! As you did to them, so I must do to you."

"Who told you that?" said Tom.

"You did yourself, this very minute."

Tom had never opened his lips; so he was very much taken aback indeed.

"Yes; every one tells me exactly what they have done wrong; and that without knowing it themselves. So there is no use trying to hide anything from me. Now go, and be a good boy, and I will put no more pebbles in your mouth, if you put none in other creatures'."

"I did not know there was any harm in it," said Tom.

"Then you know now. People continually say that to me: but I tell them, if you don't know that fire burns, that is no reason that it should not burn you; and if you don't know that dirt breeds fever, that is no reason why the fevers should not kill you. The lobster did not know that there was any harm in getting into the lobster pot; but it caught him all the same."

"Dear me," thought Tom, "she knows everything!" And so she did, indeed.

"And so, if you do not know that things are wrong, that is no reason why you should not be punished for them; though not as much, not as much, my little man" (and the lady looked very kindly, after all), "as if you did know."

"Well, you are a little hard on a poor lad," said Tom.

"Not at all; I am the best friend you ever had in all your life. But I will tell you; I cannot help punishing people when they do wrong. I like it no more than they do; I am often very, very sorry for them, poor things: but I cannot help it. If I tried not to do it, I should do it all the same. For I work by machinery, just like an engine; and am full of wheels and springs inside; and am wound up very carefully, so that I cannot help going."

"Was it long ago since they wound you up?" asked Tom. For he thought, the cunning little fellow, "She will run down some day: or they may forget to wind her up, as old Grimes used to forget to wind up his watch when he came in from the public-house: and then I shall be safe."

"I was wound up once and for all, so long ago that I forget all about it."

"Dear me," said Tom, "you must have been made a long time!"

"I never was made, my child; and I shall go for ever and ever; for I am as old as Eternity, and yet as young as Time."

And there came over the lady's face a very curious expression— very solemn, and very sad; and yet very, very sweet. And she looked up and away, as if she were gazing through the sea, and through the sky, at something far, far off; and as she did so, there came such a quiet, tender, patient, hopeful smile over her face, that Tom thought for the moment that she did not look ugly at all.

And Tom smiled in her face, she looked so pleasant for the moment. And the strange fairy smiled too, and said:

"Yes. You thought me very ugly just now, did you not?"

Tom hung down his head, and got very red about the ears.

"And I am very ugly. I am the ugliest fairy in the world; and I shall be, till people behave themselves as they ought to do. And then I shall grow as handsome as my sister, who is the loveliest fairy in the world; and her name is Mrs. Doasyouwouldbedoneby. So she begins where I end, and I begin where she ends; and those who will not listen to her must listen to me, as you will see. Now, all of you run away, except Tom; and he may stay and see what I am going to do. It will be a very good warning for him to begin with, before he goes to school.

"Now, Tom, every Friday I come down here and call up all who have ill-used little children, and serve them as they served the children."

And at that Tom was frightened, and crept under a stone; which made the two crabs who lived there very angry, and frightened their friend the butter-fish into flapping hysterics: but he would not move for them.

And first she called up all the doctors who give little children so much physic (they were most of them old ones; for the young ones have learnt better, all but a few army surgeons, who still fancy that a baby's inside is much like a Scotch grenadier's), and she set them all in a row; and very rueful they looked; for they knew what was coming.

And first she pulled all their teeth out; and then she bled them all round; and then she dosed them with calomel, and jalap, and senna, and brimstone and treacle; and horrible faces they made; and then she gave them a great emetic of mustard and water, and no basins; and began all over again; and that was the way she spent the morning. And by that time she was so tired, she had to go to luncheon.

And after luncheon she set to work again, and called up all the
careless nurserymaids, and stuck pins into them all over, and
wheeled them about in perambulators with tight straps across their
stomachs and their heads and arms hanging over the side, till they
were quite sick and stupid. Then she called up all cruel school-
masters—whole regiments and brigades of them; and, when she
saw them, she frowned most terribly, and set to work in earnest,
as if the best part of the day's work was to come.

And she boxed their ears, and thumped them over the head with
rulers, and smacked their hands with canes, and told them that they
told stories, and were this and that bad sort of people; and the
more they were very indignant, and stood upon their honour, and
declared they told the truth, the more she declared they were not,
and they were only telling lies; and at last she birched them all
round soundly with her great birch-rod, and set them each an
imposition of three hundred thousand lines of Hebrew to learn
by heart before she came back next Friday. And at that they all
cried and howled so, that their breaths came all up through the
sea like bubbles out of soda-water; and that is one reason of the
bubbles in the sea. And by that time she was so tired that she was
glad to stop; and, indeed, she had done a very good day's work.

Tom did not quite dislike the old lady: but he could not help
thinking her a little spiteful—and no wonder if she was, poor old
soul; for, if she has to wait to grow handsome till people do as they
would be done by, she will have to wait a very long time.

But Tom longed to ask her one question; and after all, whenever
she looked at him, she did not look cross at all; and now and then

there was a funny smile in her face, and she chuckled to herself in a way which gave Tom courage, and at last he said—

"Pray, ma'am, may I ask you a question?"

"Certainly, my little dear."

"Why don't you bring all the bad masters here, and serve them out too? The butties that knock about the poor collier boys; and all cruel master sweeps, like my master Grimes? I saw him fall into the water long ago; so I surely expected he would have been here. I'm sure he was bad enough to me."

Then the old lady looked so very stern that Tom was quite frightened, and sorry that he had been so bold. But she was not angry with him. She only answered, "I look after them all the week round; and they are in a very different place from this, because they knew that they were doing wrong."

She spoke very quietly; but there was something in her voice which made Tom tingle from head to foot, as if he had got into a shoal of sea-nettles.

"But these people," she went on, "did not know that they were doing wrong: they were only stupid and impatient; and therefore I only punish them till they become patient, and learn to use their common sense like reasonable beings. But as for

chimney-sweeps and collier boys, my
sister has set good people to stop all that
sort of thing; and very much obliged to
her I am; for if she could only stop the
cruel masters from ill-using poor children, I should grow handsome at least a
thousand years sooner. And now do you
be a good boy, and do as you would be
done by, and then, when my sister,
Mrs. Doasyouwouldbedoneby,
comes on Sunday, perhaps she
will take notice of you, and
teach you how to behave.
She understands that better
than I do." And so she went.

Tom was very glad to hear
that there was no chance of

meeting Grimes again; he determined to be a very good boy all Saturday; and he was; for he never frightened one crab, nor tickled any live corals, nor put stones into the sea-anemones' mouths, to make them fancy they had got a dinner; and, when Sunday morning came, sure enough, Mrs. Doasyouwouldbedoneby came too. Whereat all the little children began dancing and clapping their hands, and Tom danced too with all his might.

Tom saw that she was a very tall woman, as tall as her sister: but instead of being old, ugly, and stern like her, she had the sweetest, kindest, tenderest, funniest, merriest face; and she understood babies thoroughly, for she had plenty of her own, whole rows and regiments of them, and has to this day. And therefore when the children saw her, they naturally all caught hold of her, and pulled her till she sat down on a stone, and climbed into her lap, and clung round her neck, and caught hold of her hands; and then they all put their thumbs into their mouths, and began cuddling and purring like so many kittens. While those who could get nowhere else sat down on the sand, and cuddled her feet for no one, you know, wears shoes in the water except horrid old bathing-women, who are afraid of the water-babies pinching their horny toes. And Tom stood staring at them; for he could not understand what it was all about.

"And who are you, you little darling?" she said.

"Oh, that is the new baby!" they all cried, pulling their thumbs out of their mouths; "and he never had any mother," and they all put their thumbs back again, for they did not wish to lose any time.

"Then I will be his mother, and he shall have the very best place; so get out all of you, this moment."

And she took up two great armfuls of babies and threw them away, right and left, into the water. But they minded it no more than the naughty boys in Struwwelpeter minded when St. Nicholas dipped them in his inkstand; and did not even take their thumbs out of their mouths, but came paddling and wriggling back to her like so many tadpoles, till you could see nothing of her from head to foot for the swarm of little babies.

But she took Tom in her arms, and laid him in the softest place of all, and kissed him, and patted him, and talked to him, tenderly and low, such things as he had never heard before in his life; and Tom looked up into her eyes, and loved her, and loved, till he fell fast asleep from pure love.

And when he awoke, she was telling the children a story. And what story did she tell them? One story she told them, which begins every Christmas Eve, and yet never ends at all for ever and ever; and, as she went on, the children took their thumbs out of their mouths, and listened quite seriously; but not sadly at all; for she never told them anything sad; and Tom listened too, and never grew tired of listening. And he listened so long that he fell fast asleep again, and, when he woke, the lady was nursing him still.

"Don't go away," said little Tom. "This is so nice. I never had any one to cuddle me before."

"Don't go away," said all the children; "you have not sung us one song."

"Well, I have time for only one. So what shall it be?"

"The doll you lost! The doll you lost!" cried all the babies at once.

So Mrs. Doasyouwouldbedoneby sang—

"I once had a sweet little doll, dears,
    The prettiest doll in the world;
Her cheeks were so red and so white, dears,
    And her hair was so charmingly curled.
But I lost my poor little doll, dears,
    As I played in the heath one day;
And I cried for her more than a week, dears;
    But I never could find where she lay.

"I found my poor little doll, dears,
    As I played in the heath one day:
Folks say she is terribly changed, dears,
    For her paint is all washed away,
And her arm trodden off by the cows, dears,
    And her hair not the least bit curled:
Yet for old sakes' sake she is still, dears,
    The prettiest doll in the world."

"And now," said she to Tom, "will you be a good boy for my sake, and torment no more sea-beasts, till I come back?"

"And you will cuddle me again?" said poor little Tom.

"Of course I will, you little duck. I should like to take you with me, and cuddle you all the way, only I must not;" and away she went.

So Tom really tried to be a good boy, and tormented no sea-beasts after that, as long as he lived.

CHAPTER VI

CHAPTER VI

Hᴇʀᴇ I ᴄᴏᴍᴇ ᴛᴏ the very saddest part of all my story. You may fancy that Tom was quite good, when he had everything that he could want or wish: but you would be very much mistaken. For he grew so fond of the sea-bull's-eyes and sea-lollipops, that his foolish little head could think of nothing else: and he was always longing for more, and wondering when Mrs. Bedonebyasyoudid would come again and give him some, and what she would give him, and how much, and whether she would give him more than the others. And he thought of nothing but lollipops by day, and dreamt of nothing else by night—and what happened then?

That he began to watch to see where she kept the sweet things; and began hiding, and sneaking, and following her about, and pretending to be looking the other way, or going after something else, till be found out that she kept them in a beautiful mother-of-pearl cabinet, away in a deep crack of the rocks.

And he longed to go to the cabinet, and yet he was afraid; and then he longed again, and was less afraid; and at last, by continual thinking about it, he longed so violently, that he was not afraid at all. And one night, when all the other children were asleep, and he could not sleep for thinking of lollipops, he crept away among the rocks, and got to the cabinet, and behold! it was open.

But, when he saw all the nice things inside, instead of being delighted, he was quite frightened, and wished he had never come there. And then he would only touch them, and he did; and then he would only taste one, and he did; and then he would only eat one, and he did; and then he would only eat two, and then three, and so on; and then he was terrified lest she should come and catch him, and began gobbling them down so fast that he did not taste them, or have any pleasure in them; and then he felt sick, and would have only one more; and then only one more again; and so on till he had eaten them all up.

And all the while, close behind him, stood Mrs. Bedonebyas-youdid. She took off her spectacles, because she did not like to see too much; and in her pity she arched up her eyebrows into her very hair, and her eyes grew so wide that they would have taken in all the sorrows of the world, and filled with great big tears, as they too often do.

But all she said was—

"Ah, you poor little dear! you are just like all the rest."

But she said it to herself, and Tom neither heard nor saw her.

And what did the strange fairy do when she saw all her lollipops eaten?

Did she fly at Tom, catch him by the scruff of the neck, hold him, howk him, hump him, hurry him, poke him, pull him, pinch him, pound him, put him in the corner, shake him, slap him, set him on a cold stone to reconsider himself, and so forth?

Not a bit. You may watch her at work, if you know where to find her. But you will never see her do that. For, if she had, she knew quite well, Tom would have fought, and kicked, and bit, and said bad words, and turned again that moment into a little heathen chimney-sweep, with his hand against every man, and every man's hand against him.

Did she question him, hurry him, frighten him, threaten him, to make him confess? Not a bit. You may see her, as I said, at her work often enough, if you know where to look for her: but you will never see her do that. For if she had, she would have tempted him to tell lies in his fright; and that would have been worse for him, if possible, than even becoming a heathen chimney-sweep again.

She just said nothing at all about the matter, not even when Tom came next day with the rest for sweet things. He was horribly afraid of coming: but he was still more afraid of staying away, lest any one should suspect him. He was dreadfully afraid, too, lest there should be no sweets—as was to be expected, he having eaten them all—and lest then the fairy should inquire who had taken them. But, behold! she pulled out just as many as ever, which astonished Tom, and frightened him still more.

And, when Mrs. Bedonebyasyoudid looked him full in the face, he shook from head to foot: however, she gave him his share like the rest, and he thought within himself that she could not have found him out.

But, when he put the sweets into his mouth, he hated the taste of them; and they made him so sick, that he had to get away as fast as he could; and terribly sick he was, and very cross and unhappy, all the week after.

Then, when next week came, he had his share again; and again the fairy looked him full in the face; but more sadly than she had ever looked. And he could not bear the sweets: but took them again in spite of himself.

And, when Mrs. Doasyouwouldbedoneby came, he wanted to be cuddled like the rest; but she said very seriously:

"I should like to cuddle you; but I cannot, you are so horny and prickly."

And Tom looked at himself: and he was all over prickles, just like a sea-egg.

Which was quite natural; for you must know and believe that people's souls make their bodies, just as a snail makes its shell. And, therefore, when Tom's soul grew all prickly with naughty tempers, his body could not help growing prickly too, so that nobody would cuddle him, or play with him, or even like to look at him.

What could Tom do now, but go away and hide in a corner, and cry? For nobody would play with him, and he knew full well why.

And he was so miserable all that week that, when the ugly fairy came, and looked at him once more full in the face, more seriously and sadly than ever, he could stand it no longer, and thrust the sweetmeats away, saying, "No, I don't want any; I can't bear them now," and then burst out crying, poor little man, and told Mrs. Bedonebyasyoudid every word as it happened.

He was horribly frightened when he had done so; for he expected her to punish him very severely. But, instead, she only took him up and kissed him, which was not quite pleasant, for her chin was very bristly indeed; but he was so lonely-hearted, he thought that rough kissing was better than none.

"I will forgive you, little man," she said. "I always forgive every one the moment they tell me the truth of their own accord."

"Then you will take away all these nasty prickles?"

"That is a very different matter. You put them there yourself, and only you can take them away."

"But how can I do that?" asked Tom, crying afresh.

"Well, I think it is time for you to go to school; so I shall fetch you a schoolmistress, who will teach you how to get rid of your prickles." And so she went away.

Tom was frightened at the notion of a schoolmistress; for he thought she would certainly come with a birch-rod or a cane; but he comforted himself, at last, that she might be something like the old woman in Vendale—which she was not in the least; for, when the fairy brought her, she was the most beautiful little girl that ever was seen, with long curls floating behind her like a golden cloud, and long robes floating all round her like a silver one.

"There he is," said the fairy, "and you must teach him to be good, whether you like or not."

"I know," said the little girl; but she did not seem quite to like, for she put her finger in her mouth, and looked at Tom under her brows; and Tom put his finger to his mouth, and looked at her under his brows, for he was horribly ashamed of himself.

The little girl seemed hardly to know how to begin; and perhaps she would never have begun at all, if poor Tom had not burst out crying, and begged her to teach him to be good, and help him to cure his prickles; and at that she grew so tender-hearted, that she began teaching him as prettily as ever child was taught in the world.

So she taught Tom every day in the week; only on Sundays she always went away home, and the kind fairy took her place. And, before she had taught Tom many Sundays, his prickles had vanished quite away, and his skin was smooth and clean again.

"Dear me!" said the little girl; "why, I know you now. You are the very same little chimney-sweep who came into my bedroom."

"Dear me!" cried Tom. "And I know you, too, now. You are the very little white lady whom I saw in bed." And he jumped at her, and longed to hug and kiss her; but did not, remembering that she was a lady born; so he only jumped round and round her, till he was quite tired.

And then they began telling each other all their story—how he had got into the water, and she had fallen over the rock; and how he had swam down to the sea, and how she had flown out of the window; and how this, that, and the other, till it was all talked out: and then they both began over again, and I can't say which of the two talked fastest.

And then they set to work at their lessons again, and both liked them so well, that they went on well till seven full years were past and gone.

You may fancy that Tom was quite content and happy all those seven years; but the truth is, he was not. He had always one thing on his mind, and that was—where little Ellie went, when she went home on Sundays.

To a very beautiful place, she said.

But what was the beautiful place like, and where was it?

All that Ellie could say was, that it was worth all the rest of the world put together. And of course that only made Tom the more anxious to go likewise.

"Miss Ellie," he said, at last, "I will know why I cannot go with you when you go home, on Sundays, or I shall have no peace, and give you none either."

"You must ask the fairies that."

So when the fairy, Mrs. Bedonebyasyoudid, came next, Tom asked her.

"Little boys who are only fit to play with sea-beasts cannot go there," she said. "Those who go there must go first where they do not like, and do what they do not like, and help somebody they do not like."

"Why, did Ellie do that?"

"Ask her."

And Ellie blushed, and said, "Yes, Tom; I did not like coming here at first; I was so much happier at home, where it is always Sunday. And I was afraid of you, Tom, at first, because—because——"

"Because I was all over prickles? But I am not prickly now, am I, Miss Ellie?"

"No," said Ellie. "I like you very much now; and I like coming here, too."

"And perhaps," said the fairy, "you will learn to like going where you don't like, and helping some one that you don't like, as Ellie has."

But Tom put his finger in his mouth, and hung his head down; for he did not see that at all.

So when Mrs. Doasyouwouldbedoneby came, Tom asked her; for he thought in his little head, She is not so strict as her sister, and perhaps she may let me off more easily.

But, when he asked the second fairy, she told him just what the first did, and in the very same words.

Tom was very unhappy at that. And, when Ellie went home on Sunday, he fretted and cried all day, and did not care to listen to the fairy's stories about good children, though they were prettier than ever. Indeed, the more he overheard of them, the less he liked to listen, because they were all about children who did what they did not like, and took trouble for other people, and worked to feed their little brothers and sisters, instead of caring only for their play. And, when she began to tell a story about a holy child in old times, who was martyred by the heathen because it would not worship idols, Tom could bear no more, and ran away and hid among the rocks.

And, when Ellie came back, he was shy with her, because he fancied she looked down on him, and thought him a coward. And then he grew quite cross with her, because she was superior to him, and did what he could not do. And poor Ellie was quite surprised and sad; and at last Tom burst out crying; but he would not tell her what was really in his mind.

And all the while he was eaten up with curiosity to know where Ellie went to; so that he began not to care for his playmates, or for the sea-palace, or anything else. But perhaps that made matters all the easier for him; for he grew so discontented with everything round him, that he did not care to stay, and did not care where he went.

"Well," he said, at last, "I am so miserable here, I'll go; if only you will go with me."

"Ah!" said Ellie, "I wish I might; but the worst of it is, that the fairy says, that you must go alone, if you go at all. Now don't poke that poor crab about, Tom" (for he was feeling very naughty and mischievous), "or the fairy will have to punish you."

Tom was very nearly saying, "I don't care if she does"; but he stopped himself in time.

"I know what she wants me to do," he said, whining most dolefully. "She wants me to go after that horrid old Grimes. I don't like him, that's certain. And if I find him, he will turn me into a chimney-sweep again, I know. That's what I have been afraid of all along."

"No, he won't—I know as much as that. Nobody can turn water-babies into sweeps, or hurt them at all, as long as they are good."

"Ah," said naughty Tom, "I see what you want; you are persuading me all along to go, because you are tired of me, and want to get rid of me."

Little Ellie opened her eyes very wide at that, and they were all brimming over with tears.

"Oh, Tom, Tom!" she said, very mournfully—and then she cried, "Oh, Tom! where are you?"

And Tom cried, "Oh, Ellie, where are you?"

For neither of them could see each other—not the least. Little Ellie vanished quite away, and Tom heard her voice calling him, and growing smaller and smaller, and fainter and fainter, till all was silent.

Who was frightened then but Tom? He swam up and down among the rocks, into all the halls and chambers, faster than ever he swam before, but could not find her. He shouted after her, but she did not answer; he asked all the other children, but they had not seen her; and at last he went up to the top of the water and began crying and screaming for Mrs. Doasyouwouldbedoneby, but she did not come. Then he began crying and screaming for Mrs. Bedonebyasyoudid—which perhaps was the best thing to do —for she came in a moment.

"Oh!" said Tom. "Oh dear, oh dear! I have been naughty to Ellie, and I have killed her—I know I have killed her."

"Not quite that," said the fairy; "but I have sent her away home, and she will not come back again for I do not know how long."

"How cruel of you to send Ellie away!" sobbed Tom. "However, I will find her again, if I go to the world's end to look for her."

Mrs. Bedonebyasyoudid did not slap Tom, and tell him to hold his tongue: but she took him on her lap very kindly, just as her sister would have done; and put him in mind how it was not her fault, because she was wound up inside, like watches, and could not help doing things whether she liked or not. And then she told him how he had been in the nursery long enough, and must go out now and see the world, if he intended ever to be a man; and how he must go all alone by himself, as every one else that ever was born has to go, and see with his own eyes, and smell with his own nose, and make his own bed and lie on it, and burn his own fingers if he put them into the fire. And then she told him how many fine things there were to be seen in the world, and what an odd, curious, pleasant, orderly, respectable, well-managed, and, on the whole, successful sort of a place it was, if people would only be tolerably brave and honest and good in it; and then she told him not to be afraid of anything he met, for nothing would harm him if he remembered all his lessons, and did what he knew was right. And at last she comforted poor little Tom so much, that he was quite eager to go, and wanted to set out that minute. "Only," he said, "if I might see Ellie once before I leave."

"Why do you want that?"

"Because—because I should be so much happier if I thought she had forgiven me."

And in the twinkling of an eye there stood Ellie, smiling, and looking so happy that Tom longed to kiss her; but was still afraid it would not be respectful.

"I am going, Ellie!" said Tom. "I am going, if it is to the world's end. But I don't like going at all, and that's the truth."

"Pooh! pooh! pooh!" said the fairy. "You will like it very well indeed, Tom, and you know that at the bottom of your heart. But if you don't, I will make you like it. Come here, and see what happens to people who do only what is pleasant."

And she took out of one of her cupboards (she had all sorts of mysterious cupboards in the cracks of the rocks) the most wonderful waterproof book, full of such photographs as never were seen. For she had found out photography (and this is a fact) more than 13,598,000 years before anybody was born. And, therefore, her photographs were very curious and famous, and the children looked with great delight for the opening of the book.

And on the title-page was written, "The History of the great and famous nation of the Doasyoulikes, who came away from the country of Hardwork, because they wanted to play on the Jew's-harp all day long."

In the first picture they saw these Doasyoulikes living in the land of Readymade, at the foot of the Happygolucky Mountains, where flapdoodle grows wild. Instead of houses, they lived in the beautiful caves of tufa, and bathed in the warm springs three times a day; and, as for clothes, it was so warm there that the gentlemen walked about in little beside a cocked hat and a pair of straps, or some light summer tackle of that kind; and the ladies all gathered gossamer in autumn (when they were not too lazy) to make their winter dresses.

They were very fond of music, but it was too much trouble to learn the piano or the violin; and, as for dancing, that would have been too great an exertion. So they sat on ant-hills all day long, and played on the Jews'-harp; and, if the ants bit them, why they just got up and went to the next ant-hill, till they were bitten there likewise.

And they sat under the flapdoodle-trees, and let the flapdoodle drop into their mouths; and under the vines, and squeezed the grape-juice down their throats; and, if any little pigs ran about ready roasted, crying, "Come and eat me," as was their fashion in that country, they waited till the pigs ran against their mouths, and then took a bite, and were content, just as so many oysters would have been.

They needed no weapons, for no enemies ever came near their land; and no tools, for everything was readymade to their hand; and the stern old fairy Necessity never came near them to hunt them up, and make them use their wits, or die.

And so on, and so on, and so on, till there were never such comfortable, easy-going, happy-go-lucky people in the world.

"Well, that is a jolly life," said Tom.

"You think so?" said the fairy. "Do you see that great peaked mountain there behind," said the fairy, "with smoke coming out of its top?"

"Yes."

"And do you see all those ashes, and slag, and cinders lying about?"

"Yes."

"Then turn over the next five hundred years, and you will see what happens next."

And behold the mountain had blown up like a barrel of

gunpowder, and then boiled over like a kettle; whereby one-third of the Doasyoulikes were blown into the air, and another third were smothered in ashes; so that there was only one-third left.

"You see," said the fairy, "what comes of living on a burning mountain."

"Oh, why did you not warn them?" said little Ellie.

"I did warn them all that I could. I let the smoke come out of the mountain; and wherever there is smoke there is fire. And I laid the ashes and cinders all about; and wherever there are cinders, cinders may be again. But they did not like to face facts, my dears, as very few people do; and so they invented a cock-and-bull story, which, I am sure, I never told them, that the smoke was the breath of a giant, whom some gods or other had buried under the mountain; and that the cinders were what the dwarfs roasted the little pigs whole with; and other nonsense of that kind. And, when folks are in that humour, I cannot teach them, save by the good old birch-rod."

And then she turned over the next five hundred years: and there were the remnant of the Doasyoulikes, doing as they liked, as before. They were too lazy to move away from the mountain; so they said, If it has blown up once, that is all the more reason that it should not blow up again. And they were few in number: but they only said, The more the merrier, but the fewer the better fare. However, that was not quite true; for all the flapdoodle-trees were killed by the volcano, and they had eaten all the roast pigs, who, of course, could not be expected to have little ones. So they had to live very hard, on nuts and roots which they scratched out of the ground with sticks. Some of them talked of sowing corn, as their ancestors used to do, before they came into the land of Readymade; but they had forgotten how to make ploughs (they had forgotten even how to make Jews'-harps by this time), and had eaten all the seed-corn which they brought out of the land of Hardwork years since; and of course it was too much trouble to go away and find more. So they lived miserably on roots and nuts, and all the weakly little children had great stomachs, and then died.

"Why," said Tom, "they are growing no better than savages."

"And look how ugly they are all getting," said Ellie.

"Yes; when people live on poor vegetables instead of roast beef and plum-pudding, their jaws grow large, and their lips grow coarse."

And she turned over the next five hundred years. And there they were all living up in trees, and making nests to keep off the rain. And underneath the trees lions were prowling about.

"Why," said Ellie, "the lions seem to have eaten a good many of them, for there are very few left now."

"Yes," said the fairy; "you see it was only the strongest and most active ones who could climb the trees, and so escape."

"But what great, hulking, broad-shouldered chaps they are," said Tom; "they are a rough lot as ever I saw."

"Yes, they are getting very strong now; for the ladies will not marry any but the very strongest and fiercest gentlemen, who can help them up the trees out of the lions' way."

And she turned over the next five hundred years. And in that they were fewer still, and stronger, and fiercer; but their feet had changed shape very oddly, for they laid hold of the branches with their great toes, as if they had been thumbs, just as a Hindoo tailor uses his toes to thread his needle.

The children were very much surprised, and asked the fairy whether that was her doing.

"Yes, and no," she said, smiling. "It was only those who could use their feet as well as their hands who could get a good living: or, indeed, get married; so that they got the best of everything and starved out all the rest; and those who are left keep up a regular breed of toe-thumb-men, as a breed of shorthorns, or skye-terriers, or fancy pigeons is kept up."

"But there is a hairy one among them," said Ellie.

"Ah!" said the fairy, "that will be a great man in his time, and chief of all the tribe."

And, when she turned over the next five hundred years, it was true.

For this hairy chief had had hairy children, and they hairier children still; and every one wished to marry hairy husbands, and have hairy children too; for the climate was growing so damp that none but the hairy ones could live: all the rest coughed and sneezed, and had sore throats, and went into consumptions, before they could grow up to be men and women.

Then the fairy turned over the next five hundred years. And they were fewer still.

"Why, there is one on the ground picking up roots," said Ellie, "and he cannot walk upright."

No more he could; for in the same way that the shape of their feet had altered, the shape of their backs had altered also.

"Why," cried Tom, "I declare they are all apes."

"Something fearfully like it, poor foolish creatures," said the fairy. "They are grown so stupid now, that they can hardly think: for none of them have used their wits for many hundred years. They have almost forgotten, too, how to talk. For each stupid child forgot some of the words it heard from its stupid parents, and had not wits enough to make fresh words for itself. Beside, they are grown so fierce and suspicious and brutal that they keep out of each other's way, and mope and sulk in the dark forests, never hearing each other's voice, till they have forgotten almost what speech is like. I am afraid they will all be apes very soon, and all by doing only what they liked."

And in the next five hundred years they were all dead and gone, by bad food and wild beasts and hunters; all except one tremendous old fellow with jaws like a jack, who stood full seven feet high. And when a hunter came and shot him, he remembered that his ancestors had once been men, and tried to say, "Am I not a man and a brother?" but had forgotten how to use his tongue; and then he had tried to call for a doctor, but he had forgotten the word for one. So all he said was, "Ubboboo!" and died.

And that was the end of the great and jolly nation of the Doasyoulikes. And, when Tom and Ellie came to the end of the book, they looked very sad and solemn.

"But could you not have saved them from becoming apes?" said little Ellie, at last.

"At first, my dear; if only they would have behaved like men, and set to work to do what they did not like. But the longer they waited, and behaved like the dumb beasts, who only do what they like, the stupider and clumsier they grew; till at last they were past all cure, for they had thrown their own wits away. It is such things as this that help to make me so ugly, that I know not when I shall grow fair."

"And where are they all now?" asked Ellie.

"Exactly where they ought to be, my dear."

"Yes!" said the fairy, solemnly, half to herself, as she closed the wonderful book. "Folks say now that I can make beasts into men, by circumstance, and selection, and competition, and so forth. Well, perhaps they are right; and perhaps, again, they are wrong. That is one of the seven things which I am forbidden to tell, till the coming of the Cocqcigrues; and, at all events, it is no concern of theirs. Whatever their ancestors were, men they are; and I advise them to behave as such, and act accordingly. But let them recollect this, that there are two sides to every question, and a downhill as well as an uphill road; and, if I can turn beasts into men, I can, by the same laws of circumstance, and selection, and competition, turn men into beasts. You were very near being turned into a beast once or twice, little Tom. Indeed, if you had not made up your mind to go on this journey, and see the world, I am not sure but that you would have ended as an eft in a pond."

"Oh, dear me!" said Tom; "sooner than that, and be all over slime, I'll go this minute, if it is to the world's end."

CHAPTER VII

CHAPTER VII

"Now," said Tom, "I am ready to be off, if it's to the world's end."

"Ah!" said the fairy, "that is a brave, good boy. But you must go further than the world's end, if you want to find Mr. Grimes; for he is at the Other-end-of-Nowhere. You must go to Shiny Wall, and through the white gate that never was opened; and then you will come to Peacepool, and Mother Carey's Haven, where the good whales go when they die. And there Mother Carey will tell you the way to the Other-end-of-Nowhere, and there you will find Mr. Grimes."

"Oh, dear!" said Tom. "But I do not know my way to Shiny Wall, or where it is at all."

"Little boys must take the trouble to find out things for themselves, or they will never grow to be men; so that you must ask all the beasts in the sea and the birds in the air, and if you have been good to them, some of them will tell you the way to Shiny Wall."

"Well," said Tom, "it will be a long journey, so I had better start at once. Good-bye, Miss Ellie; you know I am getting a big boy, and I must go out and see the world."

"I know you must," said Ellie; "but you will not forget me, Tom. I shall wait here till you come."

And she shook hands with him, and bade him goodbye. Tom promised not to forget her: but his little whirl-about of a head was so full of the notion of going out to see the world, that it forgot her in five minutes: however, though his head forgot her, his heart did not.

So he asked all the beasts in the sea, and all the birds in the air, but none of them knew the way to Shiny Wall. For why? He was still too far down south.

Then he met a ship, far larger than he had ever seen—a gallant ocean-steamer, with a long cloud of smoke trailing behind; and he wondered how she went on without sails, and swam up to her to see. A school of dolphins were running races round and round her, going three feet for her one, and Tom asked them the way to Shiny Wall: but they did not know. Then he tried to find out how she moved, and at last he saw her screw, and was so delighted with it that he played under her quarter all day, till he nearly had his nose knocked off by the fans, and thought it time to move. Then he watched the sailors upon deck, and the ladies, with their bonnets and parasols: but none of them could see him, because their eyes were not opened—as, indeed, most people's eyes are not.

At last there came out into the quarter-gallery a very pretty lady, in deep black widow's weeds, and in her arms a baby. She leaned over the quarter-gallery, and looked back and back toward England far away; and as she looked she began to sing.

Her voice was so soft and low, and the music of the air so sweet, that Tom could have listened to it all day. But as she held the baby over the gallery-rail, to show it the dolphins leaping and the water gurgling in the ship's wake, lo! and behold, the baby saw Tom.

He was quite sure of that; for when their eyes met, the baby smiled and held out its hands; and Tom smiled and held out his hands too; and the baby kicked and leaped, as if it wanted to jump overboard to him.

"What do you see, my darling?" said the lady; and her eyes followed the baby's till she too caught sight of Tom, swimming about among the foam-beads below.

She gave a little shriek and start; and then she said, quite quietly, "Babies in the sea? Well, perhaps it is the happiest place for them," and waved her hand to Tom, and cried, "Wait a little, darling, only a little: and perhaps we shall go with you and be at rest."

And at that an old nurse, all in black, came out and talked to her, and drew her in. And Tom turned away northward, sad and wondering; and watched the great steamer slide away into the dusk, and the lights on board peep out one by one, and die out again, and the long bar of smoke fade away into the evening mist, till all was out of sight.

And he swam northward again, day after day, till at last he met the King of the Herrings, with a currycomb growing out of his nose, and a sprat in his mouth for a cigar, and asked him the way to Shiny Wall; so he bolted his sprat headforemost, and said:

"If I were you, young gentleman, I should go to the Allalone-stone, and ask the last of the Gairfowl. She is of a very ancient clan, very nearly as ancient as my own; and knows a good deal which these modern upstarts don't, as ladies of old houses are likely to do."

And the King of the Herrings told him the way very kindly; for he was a courteous old gentleman of the old school.

But just as Tom had thanked him and set off, he called after him: "Hi! I say, can you fly?"

"I never tried," says Tom. "Why?"

"Because, if you can, I should advise you to say nothing to the old lady about it. There; take a hint. Good-bye."

And away Tom went for seven days and seven nights due north-west, till he came to a great codbank, the like of which he never saw before. The great cod lay below in tens of thousands, and gobbled shell-fish all day long; and the blue sharks roved above in hundreds, and gobbled them when they came up. So they ate, and ate, and ate each other, as they had done since the making of the world; for no man had come here yet to catch them, and find out how rich old Mother Carey is.

And there he saw the last of the Gairfowl, standing up on the Allalonestone, all alone. And a very grand old lady she was, full three feet high, and bolt upright, like some old Highland chieftainess. She had on a black velvet gown, and a white pinner and apron, and a very high bridge to her nose (which is a sure mark of high breeding), and a large pair of white spectacles on it, which made her look rather odd: but it was the ancient fashion of her house.

And instead of wings, she had two little feathery arms, with which she fanned herself, and complained of the dreadful heat; and she kept on crooning an old song to herself, which she learned when she was a little baby-bird, long ago:

"Two little birds, they sat on a stone,
One swam away, and then there was one;
With a fal-lal-la-lady.

"The other swam after, and then there was none,
   And so the poor stone was left all alone;
      With a fal-lal-la-lady."

It was "flew" away, properly, and not "swam" away: but, as she could not fly, she had a right to alter it. However, it was a very fit song for her to sing, because she was a lady herself.

Tom came up to her very humbly, and made his bow; and the first thing she said was:

"Have you wings? Can you fly?"

"Oh dear, no, ma'am; I should not think of such a thing," said cunning little Tom.

"Then I shall have great pleasure in talking to you, my dear. It is quite refreshing nowadays to see anything without wings. They must all have wings, forsooth, now, every new upstart sort of bird, and fly. What can they want with flying, and raising themselves above their proper station in life? In the days of my ancestors no birds ever thought of having wings, and did very well without; and now they all laugh at me because I keep to the good old fashion. Why, the very marrocks and dovekies have got wings, the vulgar creatures, and poor little ones enough they are; and my own cousins too, the razor-bills, who are gentlefolk born, and ought to know better than to ape their inferiors."

And so she was running on, while Tom tried to get in a word edgeways; and at last he did, when the old lady got out of breath, and began fanning herself again; and then he asked if she knew the way to Shiny Wall.

"Shiny Wall? Who should know better than I? We all came from Shiny Wall, thousands of years ago, when it was decently cold, and the climate was fit for gentlefolk; but now, what with the heat, and what with these vulgar-winged things who fly up and down and eat everything, so that gentle-people's hunting is all spoilt, and one really cannot get one's living, or hardly venture off the rock for fear of being flown against by some creature that would not have dared to come within a mile of one a thousand years ago—what was I saying? Why, we have quite gone down in the world, my dear, and have nothing left but our honour. And I am the last of my family. A friend of mine and I came and settled on this rock when we were young, to be out of the way of low people. Once we were a great nation, and spread over all the Northern Isles. But men shot us so, and knocked us on the head, and took our eggs—why, if you will believe it, they say that on the coast of Labrador the sailors used to lay a plank from the rock on board the thing they called their ship, and drive us along the plank by hundreds, till we tumbled down into the ship's waist in heaps; and then, I suppose, they ate us, the nasty fellows! Well—but—what was I saying? At last there were none of us left, except on the old Gairfowlskerry, just off the Iceland coast, up which no man could climb. Even there we had no peace; for one day, when I was quite a young girl, the land rocked, and the sea boiled, and the sky grew dark, and all the air was filled with smoke and dust, and down tumbled the old Gairfowlskerry into the sea. The dovekies and marrocks, of course, all flew away; but we were too proud to do that. Some of us were dashed to pieces, and some drowned; and those who were left got away to Eldey, and the dovekies tell me they are all dead now, and that another Gairfowlskerry has risen out of the sea close to the old one, but that it is such a poor flat place that it is not safe to live on: and so here I am left alone. And soon I shall be gone, my little dear, and nobody will miss me; and then the poor stone will be left all alone."

"But, please, which is the way to Shiny Wall?" said Tom.

"Oh, you must go, my little dear—you must go. Let me see—I am sure—that is—really, my poor old brains are getting quite puzzled. Do you know, my little dear, I am afraid, if you want to know, you must ask some of these vulgar birds about, for I have quite forgotten."

And the poor old Gairfowl began to cry tears of pure oil; and Tom was quite sorry for her; and for himself too, for he was at his wit's end whom to ask.

But by there came a flock of petrels, who are Mother Carey's own chickens; and Tom thought them much prettier than Lady Gairfowl, and so perhaps they were; for Mother Carey had had a great deal of fresh experience between the time that she invented the Gairfowl and the time that she invented them. They flitted along like a flock of black swallows, and hopped and skipped from wave to wave, lifting up their little feet behind them so daintily, and whistling to each other so tenderly, that Tom fell in love with them at once, and called them to know the way to Shiny Wall.

"Shiny Wall? Do you want Shiny Wall? Then come with us, and we will show you. We are Mother Carey's own chickens, and she sends us out over all the seas, to show the good birds the way home."

Tom was delighted, and swam off to them, after he had made his bow to the Gairfowl. But she would not return his bow: but held herself bolt upright, and wept tears of oil as she sang:

"And so the poor stone was left all alone;
    With a fal-lal-la-lady."

And now Tom was all agog to start for Shiny Wall; but the petrels said no. They must go first to Allfowlsness, and wait there for the great gathering of all the seabirds, before they start for their summer breeding-places far away in the Northern isles; and

there they would be sure to find some birds which were going to
Shiny Wall: but where Allfowlsness was, he must promise never
to tell, lest men should go there and shoot the birds, and stuff
them, and put them into stupid museums, instead of leaving them
to play and breed and work in Mother Carey's water-garden,
where they ought to be.

So where Allfowlsness is nobody must know; and all that is to
be said about it is, that Tom waited there many days.

And after a while the birds began to gather at Allfowlsness, in
thousands and tens of thousands, blackening all the air; swans and
brant geese, harlequins and eiders, harelds and garganeys, smews
and goosanders, divers and loons, grebes and dovekies, auks and
razorbills, gannets and petrels, skuas and terns, with gulls beyond
all naming or numbering; and they paddled and washed and
splashed and combed and brushed themselves on the sand, till the
shore was white with feathers; and they quacked and clucked
and gabbled and chattered and screamed and whooped as they
talked over matters with their friends, and settled where they were
to go and breed that summer, till you might have heard them ten
miles off; and lucky it was for them that there was no one to hear
them but the old keeper, who lived all alone upon the Ness, in a
turf hut thatched with heather and fringed round with great
stones slung across the roof by bent-ropes, lest the winter gales
should blow the hut right away. But he never minded the birds
nor hurt them, because they were not in season: indeed, he
minded but two things in the whole world, and those were, his
Bible and his grouse; for he was as good an old Scotchman as

ever knit stockings on a winter's night: only, when all the birds were going, he toddled out, and took off his cap to them, and wished them a merry journey and a safe return; and then gathered up all the feathers which they had left, and cleaned them to sell down south, and make feather-beds for stuffy people to lie on.

Then the petrels asked this bird and that whether they would take Tom to Shiny Wall: but one set was going to Sutherland, and one to the Shetlands, and one to Norway, and one to Spitzbergen, and one to Iceland, and one to Greenland; but none would go to Shiny Wall. So the good-natured petrels said that they would show him part of the way themselves, but they were only going as far as Jan Mayen's land; and after that he must shift for himself.

And then all the birds rose up, and streamed away in long black lines, north, and north-east, and north-west, across the bright blue summer sky; and their cry was like ten thousand packs of hounds, and ten thousand peals of bells. Only the puffins stayed behind, and killed the young rabbits, and laid their eggs in the rabbit-burrows; which was rough practice, certainly: but a man must see to his own family.

And, as Tom and the petrels went north-eastward, it began to blow right hard; for the old gentleman in the grey great-coat, who looks after the big copper boiler in the gulf of Mexico, had got behind-hand with his work; so Mother Carey had sent an electric message to him for more steam; and now the steam was coming, as much in an hour as ought to have come in a week, puffing and roaring and swishing and swirling, till you could not see where the sky ended and the sea began. But Tom and the petrels never cared, for the gale was right abaft, and away they went over the crests of the billows, as merry as so many flying-fish.

And at last they saw an ugly sight—the black side of a great ship, water-logged in the trough of the sea. Her funnel and her masts were overboard, and swayed and surged under her lee; her decks were swept as clean as a barn floor, and there was no living soul on board.

The petrels flew up to her, and wailed round her; for they were very sorry indeed, and also they expected to find some salt pork; and Tom scrambled on board of her and looked round, frightened and sad.

And there, in a little cot, lashed tight under the bulwark, lay a baby fast asleep; the very same baby, Tom saw at once, which he had seen in the singing lady's arms.

He went up to it, and wanted to wake it: but behold, from under the cot out jumped a little black and tan terrier dog, and began barking and snapping at Tom, and would not let him touch the cot.

Tom knew the dog's teeth could not hurt him: but at least it could shove him away, and did; and he and the dog fought and struggled, for he wanted to help the baby, and did not want to throw the poor dog overboard; but, as they were struggling, there came a tall green sea, and walked in over the weather side of the ship, and swept them all into the waves.

"Oh, the baby, the baby!" screamed Tom: but the next moment he did not scream at all; for he saw the cot settling down through the green water, with the baby smiling in it, fast asleep; and he saw the fairies come up from below, and carry baby and cradle gently down in their soft arms; and then he knew it was all right, and that there would be a new water-baby in St. Brandan's Isle.

And the poor little dog?

Why, after he had kicked and coughed a little, he sneezed so hard, that he sneezed himself clean out of his skin, and turned into a water-dog, and jumped and danced round Tom, and ran over the crests of the waves, and snapped at the jelly-fish and the mackerel, and followed Tom the whole way to the Other-end-of-Nowhere.

Then they went on again, till they began to see the peak of Jan Mayen's Land, standing up like a white sugar-loaf, two miles above the clouds.

And there they fell in with a whole flock of mollymocks, who were feeding on a dead whale.

"These are the fellows to show you the way," said Mother Carey's chickens; "we cannot help you further north. We don't like to get among the ice pack, for fear it should nip our toes; but the mollys dare fly anywhere."

So the petrels called to the mollys: but they were so busy and greedy, gobbling and pecking and spluttering and fighting over the blubber, that they did not take the least notice.

"Come, come," said the petrels, "you lazy greedy lubbers, this young gentleman is going to Mother Carey, and if you don't attend on him, you won't earn your discharge from her, you know."

"Greedy we are," says a great fat old molly, "but lazy we ain't; and, as for lubbers, we're no more lubbers than you. Let's have a look at the lad."

And he flapped right into Tom's face, and stared at him in the most impudent way (for the mollys are audacious fellows, as all whalers know), and then asked him where he hailed from, and what land he sighted last.

And, when Tom told him, he seemed pleased, and said he was a good-plucked one to have got so far.

"Come along, lads," he said to the rest, "and give this little chap a cast over the pack, for Mother Carey's sake. We've eaten blubber enough for to-day, and we'll e'en work out a bit of our time by helping the lad."

So the mollys took Tom up on their backs, and flew off with

him, laughing and joking—and oh, how they did smell of train oil!

"Who are you, you jolly birds?" asked Tom.

"We are the spirits of the old Greenland skippers (as every sailor knows), who hunted here, right whales and horse-whales, full hundreds of years agone. But, because we were saucy and greedy, we were all turned into mollys, to eat whale's blubber all our days. But lubbers we are none, and could sail a ship now against any man in the North Seas, though we don't hold with this new-fangled steam. And it's a shame of those black imps of petrels to call us so; but because they're her grace's pets, they think they may say anything they like."

"And who are you?" asked Tom of him, for he saw that he was the king of all the birds.

"My name is Hendrick Hudson, and a right good skipper was I; and my name will last to the world's end, in spite of all the wrong I did. For I discovered Hudson River, and I named Hudson's Bay; and many have come in my wake that dared not have shown me the way. But I was a hard man in my time, that's truth, and stole the poor Indians off the coast of Maine, and sold them for slaves down in Virginia; and at last I was so cruel to my sailors, here in these very seas, that they set me adrift in an open boat, and I never was heard of more. So now I'm the king of all the mollys, till I've worked out my time."

And now they came to the edge of the pack, and beyond it they could see Shiny Wall looming, through mist, and snow, and storm. But the pack rolled horribly upon the swell, and the ice giants fought and roared, and leaped upon each other's backs, and ground each other to powder, so that Tom was afraid to venture among them, lest he should be ground to powder too. And he was the more afraid, when he saw lying among the ice pack the wrecks of many a gallant ship; some with masts and yards all standing, some with the seamen frozen fast on board. Alas, alas, for them! They were all true English hearts; and they came to their end like good knights-errant, in searching for the white gate that never was opened yet.

But the good mollys took Tom and his dog up, and flew with them safe over the pack and the roaring ice giants, and set them down at the foot of Shiny Wall.

"And where is the gate?" asked Tom.

"There is no gate," said the mollys.

"No gate?" cried Tom, aghast.

"None; never a crack of one, and that's the whole of the secret, as better fellows, lad, than you have found to their cost; and if there had been, they'd have killed by now every right whale that swims the sea."

"What am I to do, then?"

"Dive under the floe, to be sure, if you have pluck."

"I've not come so far to turn now," said Tom; "so here goes for a header."

"A lucky voyage to you, lad," said the mollys; "we knew you were one of the right sort. So good-bye."

"Why don't you come too?" asked Tom.

But the mollys only wailed sadly, "We can't go yet, we can't go yet," and flew away over the pack.

So Tom dived under the great white gate which never was opened yet, and went on in black darkness, at the bottom of the sea, for seven days and seven nights.

And at last he saw the light, and clear clear water over head; and up he came a thousand fathoms, among clouds of sea-moths, which fluttered round his head. There were moths with pink heads and wings and opal bodies, that flapped about slowly; moths with brown wings that flapped about quickly; yellow shrimps that hopped and skipped most quickly of all; and jellies of all the colours in the world, that neither hopped nor skipped, but only dawdled and yawned, and would not get out of his way. The dog snapped at them till his jaws were tired: but Tom hardly minded them at all, he was so eager to get to the top of the water, and see the pool where the good whales go.

And a very big pool it was, miles and miles across, though the air was so clear that the ice cliffs on the opposite side looked as if they were close at hand. All round it the ice cliffs rose, in walls and spires and battlements, and caves and bridges, and stories and galleries, in which the ice-fairies live, and drive away the storms and clouds, that Mother Carey's pool may lie calm from year's end to year's end. And the sun acted policeman, and walked round outside every day, peeping just over the top of the ice wall, to see that all went right; and now and then he played conjuring tricks, or had an exhibition of fireworks, to amuse the ice-fairies. For he would make himself into four or five suns at once, or paint the sky with rings and crosses and crescents of white fire, and stick himself in the middle of them, and wink at the fairies; and I dare say they were very much amused; for anything's fun in the country.

And there the good whales lay, the happy sleepy beasts, upon the still oily sea. They were all right whales, you must know, and finners, and razor-backs, and bottle-noses, and spotted sea-unicorns with long ivory horns. But the sperm whales are such raging, ramping, roaring, rumbustious fellows, that, if Mother Carey let them in, there would be no more peace in Peacepool. So she packs them away in a great pond by themselves at the South Pole, two hundred and sixty-three miles south-south-east of Mount Erebus, the great volcano in the ice; and there they butt each other with their ugly noses, day and night from year's end to year's end.

But here there were only good quiet beasts, lying about like the black hulls of sloops, and blowing every now and then jets of white steam, or sculling round with their huge mouths open, for the sea-moths to swim down their throats. There were no threshers there to thresh their poor old backs, or sword-fish to stab their stomachs, or saw-fish to rip them up, or ice-sharks to bite lumps out of their sides, or whalers to harpoon and lance them. They were quite safe and happy there; and all they had to do was to wait quietly in Peacepool, till Mother Carey sent for them to make them out of old beasts into new.

Tom swam up to the nearest whale, and asked the way to Mother Carey.

"There she sits in the middle," said the whale.

Tom looked; but he could see nothing in the middle of the pool but one peaked iceberg: and he said so.

"That's Mother Carey," said the whale, "as you will find when you get to her. There she sits making old beasts into new all the year round."

"How does she do that?"

"That's her concern, not mine," said the old whale; and yawned so wide (for he was very large) that there swam into his mouth 943 sea-moths, 13,846 jelly-fish no bigger than pin's heads, a string of salpæ nine yards long, and forty-three little ice-crabs, who gave each other a parting pinch all round, tucked their legs under their stomachs, and determined to die decently, like Julius Cæsar.

"I suppose," said Tom, "she cuts up a great whale like you into a whole shoal of porpoises?"

At which the old whale laughed so violently that he coughed up all the creatures; who swam away again very thankful at having escaped out of that terrible whalebone net of his, from which bourne no traveller returns; and Tom went on to the iceberg, wondering.

And, when he came near it, it took the form of the grandest old lady he had ever seen—a white marble lady, sitting on a white marble throne. And from the foot of the throne there swum away, out and out into the sea, millions of new-born creatures, of more shapes and colours than man ever dreamed. And they were Mother Carey's children, whom she makes out of the sea-water all day long.

She sat quite still with her chin upon her hand, looking down into the sea with two great grand blue eyes, as blue as the sea itself. Her hair was as white as the snow—for she was very very old—in fact, as old as anything which you are likely to come across, except the difference between right and wrong.

And, when she saw Tom, she looked at him very kindly.

"What do you want, my little man? It is long since I have seen a water-baby here."

Tom told her his errand, and asked the way to the Other-end-of-Nowhere.

"You ought to know yourself, for you have been there already."

"Have I, ma'am? I'm sure I forget all about it."

"Then look at me."

And, as Tom looked into her great blue eyes, he recollected the way perfectly.

Now, was not that strange?

"Thank you, ma'am," said Tom. "Then I won't trouble your ladyship any more; I hear you are very busy."

"I am never more busy than I am now," she said, without stirring a finger.

"I heard, ma'am, that you were always making new beasts out of old."

"So people fancy. But I am not going to trouble myself to make things, my little dear. I sit here and make them make themselves. Any one can make things, if they will take time and trouble enough: but it is not every one who, like me, can make things make themselves."

"You are a clever fairy, indeed," thought Tom. And he was quite right.

"And now, my little man," said Mother Carey, "you are sure you know the way to the Other-end-of-Nowhere?"

Tom thought; and behold, he had forgotten it utterly.

"That is because you took your eyes off me."

Tom looked at her again, and recollected; and then looked away, and forgot in an instant.

"But what am I to do, ma'am? For I can't keep looking at you when I am somewhere else."

"You must do without me, as most most people have to do, for nine hundred and ninety-nine thousandths of their lives; and look at the dog instead; for he knows the way well enough, and will not forget it. Besides, you may meet some very queer-tempered people there, who will not let you pass without this passport of mine, which you must hang round your neck and take care of; and, of course, as the dog will always go behind you, you must go the whole way backward."

"Backward!" cried Tom. "Then I shall not be able to see my way."

"On the contrary, if you look forward, you will not see a step before you, and be certain to go wrong; but, if you look behind you, and watch carefully whatever you have passed, and especially keep your eye on the dog, who goes by instinct, and therefore can't go wrong, then you will know what is coming next as plainly as if you saw it in a looking-glass."

Tom was very much astonished: but he obeyed her, for

he had learned always to believe what the fairies told him.

Tom was very sorely tried; for though, by keeping the dog to heels (or rather to toes, for he had to walk backward), he could see pretty well which way the dog was hunting, yet it was much slower work to go backwards than to go forwards. But, what was more trying still, no sooner had he got out of Peacepool, than there came running to him all the conjurors, fortune-tellers, astrologers, prophesiers, projectors, prestigiators, as many as were in those parts (and there are too many of them everywhere) all bawling and screaming at him, "Look a-head, only look a-head; and we will show you what man never saw before, and right away to the end of the world!"

But Tom was such a little dogged, hard, gnarly, foursquare brick of a boy, that he never turned his head round once all the way from Peacepool to the Other-end-of-Nowhere: but kept his eye on the dog, and let him pick out the scent, hot or cold, straight or crooked, wet or dry, up hill or down dale; by which means he never made a single mistake, and saw all the wonderful and hitherto by-no-mortal-man-imagined things, which are related in the next chapter.

CHAPTER VIII

CHAPTER VIII AND LAST

Now as soon as Tom had left Peacepool he came to the white lap of the great sea-mother, ten thousand fathoms deep; where she makes world-pap all day long, for the steam-giants to knead, and the fire-giants to bake, till it has risen and hardened into mountain-loaves and island-cakes.

And there Tom was very near being kneaded up in the world-pap, and turned into a fossil water-baby; which would have astonished the Geological Society of New Zealand some hundreds of thousands of years hence.

For, as he walked along in the silence of the sea-twilight, on the soft white ocean floor, he was aware of a hissing, and a roaring, and a thumping, and a pumping, as of all the steam-engines in the world at once. And, when he came near, the water grew boiling hot; not that that hurt him in the least: but it also grew as foul as gruel; and every moment he stumbled over dead shells, and fish, and sharks, and seals, and whales, which had been killed by the hot water.

And at last he came to the great sea-serpent himself, lying dead at the bottom; and, as he was too thick to scramble over, Tom had to walk round him three-quarters of a mile and more, which put him out of his path sadly; and, when he had got round, he came to the place called Stop. And there he stopped, and just in time.

For he was on the edge of a vast hole in the bottom of the sea, up which was rushing and roaring clear steam enough to work all the engines in the world at once; so clear, indeed, that it was quite light at moments; and Tom could see almost up to the top of the water above, and down below into the pit for nobody knows how far.

But, as soon as he bent his head over the edge, he got such a rap on the nose from pebbles, that he jumped back again; for the steam, as it rushed up, rasped away the sides of the hole, and hurled it up into the sea in a shower of mud and gravel and ashes; and it spread all around, and sank again, and covered in the dead fish so fast, that before Tom had stood there five minutes he was buried in silt up to his ankles, and began to be afraid that he should have been buried alive.

And perhaps he would have been, but that while he was thinking, the whole piece of ground on which he stood was torn off and blown upwards, and away flew Tom a mile up through the sea, wondering what was coming next.

At last he stopped—thump! and found himself tight in the legs of the most wonderful bogy which he had ever seen.

It had I don't know how many wings, as big as the sails of a windmill, and spread out in a ring like them; and with them it hovered over the steam which rushed up, as a ball hovers over the top of a fountain. And for every wing above it had a leg below, with a claw like a comb at the tip, and a nostril at the root; and in the middle it had no stomach and one eye; and as for its mouth, that was all on one side, as the madreporiform tubercle in a starfish

is. Well, it was a very strange beast; but no stranger than some dozens which you may see.

"What do you want here," it cried quite peevishly, "getting in my way?" and it tried to drop Tom: but he held on tight to its claws, thinking himself safer where he was.

So Tom told him who he was, and what his errand was. And the thing winked its one eye, and sneered:

"I am too old to be taken in in that way. You are come after gold—I know you are."

"Gold! What is gold?" And really Tom did not know; but the suspicious old bogy would not believe him.

But after a while Tom began to understand a little. For, as the vapours came up out of the hole, the body smelt them with his nostrils, and combed them and sorted them with his combs; and then, when they steamed up through them against his wings, they were changed into showers and streams of metal. From one wing fell gold-dust, and from another silver, and from another copper, and from another tin, and from another lead, and so on, and sank into the soft mud, into veins and cracks, and hardened there. Whereby it comes to pass that the rocks are full of metal.

But, all of a sudden, somebody shut off the steam below, and the hole was left empty in an instant: and then down rushed the water into the hole, in such a whirlpool that the bogy spun round and round as fast as a tee-totum. But that was all in his day's work, like a fair fall with the hounds; so all he did was to say to Tom:

"Now is your time, youngster, to get down, if you are in earnest, which I don't believe."

"You'll soon see," said Tom; and away he went, as bold as Baron Munchausen, and shot down the rushing cataract like a salmon at Ballisodare

And, when he got to the bottom, he swam till he was washed on shore safe upon the Other-end-of-Nowhere; and he found it, to his surprise, as most other people do, much more like This-end-of-Somewhere than he had been in the habit of expecting.

And first he went through Waste-paper-land, where all the stupid books lie in heaps, up hill and down dale, like leaves in a winter wood; and there he saw people digging and grubbing among them, to make worse books out of bad ones, and thrashing chaff to save the dust of it; and a very good trade they drove thereby, especially among children.

Then he went by the sea of slops, to the mountain of messes, and the territory of tuck, where the ground was very sticky, for it was all made of bad toffee (not Everton toffee, of course), and full of deep cracks and holes choked with wind-fallen fruit, and green goose-berries, and sloes, and crabs, and whinberries, and hips and haws, and all the nasty things which little children will eat if they can get them. But the fairies hide them out of the way in that country as fast as they can, and very hard work they have, and of very little use it is. For as fast as they hide away the old trash, foolish and wicked people make fresh trash.

Next he saw all the little people in the world, writing all the little books in the world, about all the other little people in the world; probably because they had no great people to write about. And all the rest of the little people in the world read the books, and thought themselves each as good as the President; and perhaps they were right, for every one knows his own business best. But Tom thought he would sooner have a jolly good fairy tale, about Jack the Giant-killer or Beauty and the Beast, which taught him something that he didn't know already.

Then came Tom to the Island which some call Rogues' Harbour, where every one knows his neighbour's business better than his own.

There he saw ploughs drawing horses, nails driving hammers, birds' nests taking boys, books making authors, bulls keeping china-shops, monkeys shaving cats, dead dogs drilling live lions, blind brigadiers shelfed as principals of colleges, play-actors not in the least shelfed as popular preachers; and, in short, every one set to do something which he had not learned, because in what he had learned, or pretended to learn, he had failed.

When he got into the middle of the town, they all set on him at once, to show him his way; or rather, to show him that he did not know his way; for as for asking him what way he wanted to go, no one ever thought of that.

But one pulled him hither, and another poked him thither, and a third cried:

"You mustn't go west, I tell you; it is destruction to go west."

"But I am not going west, as you may see," said Tom.

And another, "The east lies here, my dear; I assure you this is the east."

"But I don't want to go east," said Tom.

"Well then at all events, whichever way you are going, you are going wrong," cried they all with one voice—which was the only thing which they ever agreed about; and all pointed at once to all the thirty-and-two points of the compass, till Tom thought all the signposts had got together, and fallen fighting.

And whether he would have ever escaped out of the town, it is hard to say, if the dog had not taken it into his head that they were going to pull his master in pieces, and tackled them so sharply that while they were rubbing their bitten calves, Tom and the dog got safe away.

On the borders of that island he found Gotham, where the wise men live; the same who dragged the pond because the moon had fallen into it, and planted a hedge round the cuckoo, to keep spring all the year. And he found them bricking up the town gate, because it was so wide that little folks could not get through.

And, when he asked why, they told him they were expanding their liturgy. So he went on; for it was no business of his: only he could not help saying that in his country, if the kitten could not get in at the same hole as the cat, she might stay outside and mew.

But he saw the end of such fellows, when he came to the island of the Golden Asses, where nothing but thistles grow. For there they were all turned into mokes with ears a yard long, for meddling with matters which they do not understand, as Lucius did in the story. And like him, mokes they must remain, till, by the laws of development, the thistles develop into roses. Till then, they must comfort themselves with the thought, that the longer their ears are, the thicker their hides; and so a good beating don't hurt them.

Then Tom came to a very famous island, which Mrs. Bedonebyasyoudid has named the Isle of Tomtoddies, all heads and no bodies.

And when Tom came near it, he heard such a grumbling and grunting and growling and wailing and weeping and whining that he thought people must be ringing little pigs, or cropping puppies' ears, or drowning kittens: but when he came nearer still, he began to hear words among the noise; which was the Tom-toddies' song which they sing morning and evening, and all night too, to their great idol Examination:

"I can't learn my lesson: the examiner's coming!"

And that was the only song which they knew.

And when Tom got on shore the first thing he saw was a great pillar, on one side of which was inscribed, "Playthings not allowed here"; at which he was so shocked that he would not stay to see what was written on the other side. Then he looked round for the people of the island: but instead of men, women, and children, he found nothing but turnips and radishes, beet and mangold wurzel, without a single green leaf among them, and half of them burst and decayed, with toadstools growing out of them. Those which were left began crying to Tom, in half a dozen different languages at once, and all of them badly spoken, "I can't learn my lesson; do come and help me!"

"And what good on earth will it do you if I did help you?" quoth Tom.

Well, they didn't know that: all they knew was the examiner was coming.

Then Tom stumbled on the hugest and softest nimble-come-quick turnip you ever saw filling a hole in a crop of swedes, and it cried to him, "Can you tell me anything at all about anything you like?"

"About what?" says Tom.

"About anything you like; for as fast as I learn things I forget them again. So my mamma says that I must go in for general information."

Tom told him that he did not know general information, nor any officers in the army; only he had a friend once that went for a drummer: but he could tell him a great many strange things which he had seen in his travels.

So he told him prettily enough, while the poor turnip listened very carefully; and the more he listened, the more he forgot, and the more water ran out of him.

Tom thought he was crying: but it was only his poor brains running away, from being worked so hard; and as Tom talked, the unhappy turnip streamed down all over with juice, and split and shrank till nothing was left of him but rind and water; whereat Tom ran away in a fright, for he thought he might be taken up for killing the turnip.

But, on the contrary, the turnip's parents were highly delighted, and considered him a saint and a martyr, and put up a long inscription over his tomb about his wonderful talents, early development, and unparalleled precocity. Were they not a foolish couple?

But there was a still more foolish couple next to them, who were beating a wretched little radish, no bigger than my thumb, for sullenness and obstinacy and wilful stupidity, and never knew that the reason why it couldn't learn or hardly even speak was, that there was a great worm inside it eating out all its brains. But even they are no foolisher than some hundred score of papas and mammas, who fetch the rod when they ought to fetch a new toy, and send to the dark cupboard instead of to the doctor.

Tom was so puzzled and frightened with all he saw, that he was longing to ask the meaning of it; and at last he stumbled over a respectable old stick lying half covered with earth.

"You see," said the stick, "they were as pretty little children once as you could wish to see, and might have been so still if they had been only left to grow up like human beings, and then handed over to me; but their foolish fathers and mothers, instead of letting them pick flowers and make dirt-pies, and get birds' nests, and dance round the gooseberry bush, as little children should, kept them always at lessons, working, working, working, learning weekday lessons all weekdays, and Sunday lessons all Sunday, and weekly examinations every Saturday, and monthly examinations every month, and yearly examinations every year, everything seven times over, as if once was not enough, and enough as good as a feast—till their brains grew big, and their bodies grew small, and they were all changed into turnips, with little but water inside; and still their foolish parents actually pick the leaves off them as fast as they grow, lest they should have anything green about them."

"Ah!" said Tom, "if dear Mrs. Doasyouwouldbedoneby knew of it she would send them a lot of tops, and balls, and marbles, and ninepins, and make them all as jolly as sand-boys."

"It would be no use," said the stick. "They can't play now, if they tried. Don't you see how their legs have turned to roots and grown into the ground, by never taking any exercise, but sapping and moping always in the same place? But here comes the Examiner-of-all-Examiners. So you had better get away, I warn you, or he will examine you and your dog into the bargain, and set him to examine all the other dogs, and you to examine all the other water-babies. There is no escaping out of his hands, for his nose is nine thousand miles long, and can go down chimneys and through keyholes, upstairs, downstairs, in my lady's chamber, examining all little boys, and the little boys' tutors likewise. But when he is thrashed—so Mrs. Bedonebyasyoudid has promised me—I shall have the thrashing of him: and if I don't lay it on with a will it's a pity."

Tom went off: but rather slowly and surlily; for he was some-what minded to face this same Examiner-of-all-Examiners. But when he got near, he looked so big and burly and dictatorial, and shouted so loud to Tom to come and be examined, that Tom ran for his life, and the dog too. And really it was time; for the poor turnips, in their hurry and fright, crammed themselves so fast to be ready for the Examiner, that they burst and popped by dozens all round him, and Tom thought he should be blown into the air, dog and all.

As he went down to the shore he passed the poor turnip's new tomb. But Mrs. Bedonebyasyoudid had taken away the epitaph about talents and precocity and development, and put up one of her own instead which Tom thought much more sensible:

> "Instruction sore long time I bore,
>   And cramming was in vain;
> Till Heaven did please my woes to ease,
>   By water on the brain."

So Tom jumped into the sea, and swam on his way. And at last, after innumerable adventures, each more wonderful than the last, he saw before him a huge building.

Tom walked towards this great building, wondering what it was, and having a strange fancy that he might find Mr. Grimes inside it, till he saw running toward him, and shouting "Stop!" three or four people, who, when they came nearer, were nothing else than policemen's truncheons, running along without legs or arms.

Tom was not astonished. He was long past that. Besides, he had seen the naviculæ in the water move nobody knows how, a hundred times, without arms, or legs, or anything to stand in their stead. Neither was he frightened; for he had been doing no harm.

So he stopped; and, when the foremost truncheon came up and asked his business, he showed Mother Carey's pass; and the truncheon looked at it in the oddest fashion; for he had one eye in the middle of his upper end, so that when he looked at anything, being quite stiff, he had to slope himself, and poke himself, till it was a wonder why he did not tumble over; but, being quite full of the spirit of justice (as all policemen, and their truncheons, ought to be), he was always in a position of stable equilibrium, whichever way he put himself.

"All right—pass on," said he at last. And then he added: "I had better go with you, young man." And Tom had no objection, for such company was both respectable and safe; so the truncheon coiled its thong neatly round its handle, to prevent tripping itself up—for the thong had got loose in running—and marched on by Tom's side.

"Why have you no policeman to carry you?" asked Tom, after a while.

"Because we are not like those clumsy-made truncheons in the land-world, which cannot go without having a whole man to carry them about. We do our own work for ourselves; and do it very well, though I say it who should not."

"Then why have you a thong to your handle?" asked Tom.

"To hang ourselves up by, of course, when we are off duty."

Tom had got his answer, and had no more to say, till they came up to the great iron door of the prison. And there the truncheon knocked twice, with its own head.

A wicket in the door opened, and out looked a tremendous old brass blunderbuss charged up to the muzzle with slugs, who was the porter; and Tom started back a little at the sight of him.

"What case is this?" he asked in a deep voice, out of his broad bell-mouth.

"If you please, sir, it is no case; only a young gentleman from her ladyship, who wants to see Grimes the master-sweep."

"Grimes?" said the blunderbuss. And he pulled in his muzzle, perhaps to look over his prison-lists.

"Grimes is up chimney No. 345," he said from inside. "So the young gentleman had better go on to the roof."

Tom looked up at the enormous wall, which seemed at least ninety miles high, and wondered how he should ever get up: but, when he hinted that to the truncheon, it settled the matter in a moment. For it whisked round, and gave him such a shove behind as sent him up to the roof in no time, with his little dog under his arm.

And there he walked along the leads, till he met another truncheon, and told him his errand.

"Very good," it said. "Come along: but it will be of no use. He is the most unremorseful, hard-hearted, foul-mouthed fellow I have in charge; and thinks about nothing but beer and pipes, which are not allowed here, of course."

So they walked along over the leads, and very sooty they were, and Tom thought the chimneys must want sweeping very much. But he was surprised to see that the soot did not stick to his feet, or dirty them in the least. Neither did the live coals, which were lying about in plenty, burn him; for he was a water-baby.

And at last they came to chimney No. 345. Out of the top of it, his head and shoulders just showing, stuck poor Mr. Grimes; so sooty, and bleared, and ugly, that Tom could hardly bear to look at him. And in his mouth was a pipe: but it was not a-light, though he was pulling at it with all his might.

"Attention, Mr. Grimes," said the truncheon; "here is a gentleman come to see you."

But Mr. Grimes only said bad words; and kept grumbling, "My pipe won't draw. My pipe won't draw."

"Keep a civil tongue, and attend!" said the truncheon; and popped up just like Punch, hitting Grimes such a crack over the head with itself, that his brains rattled inside like a dried walnut in its shell. He tried to get his hands out, and rub the place: but he could not, for they were stuck fast in the chimney.

Now he was forced to attend.

"Hey!" he said, "why, it's Tom! I suppose you have come here to laugh at me, you spiteful little atomy?"

Tom assured him he had not, but only wanted to help him.

"I don't want anything except beer, and that I can't get; and a light to this bothering pipe, and that I can't get either."

"I'll get you one," said Tom; and he took up a live coal (there were plenty lying about) and put it to Grimes's pipe: but it went out instantly.

"It's no use," said the truncheon, leaning itself up against the chimney, and looking on. "I tell you, it is no use. His heart is so cold that it freezes everything that comes near him. You will see that presently, plain enough."

"Oh, of course, it's my fault. Everything's always my fault," said Grimes. "Now don't go to hit me again" (for the truncheon started upright, and looked very wicked); "you know, if my arms were only free, you daren't hit me then."

The truncheon leaned back against the chimney, and took no notice of the personal insult, like a well-trained policeman as it was, though he was ready enough to avenge any transgression against morality or order.

"But can't I help you in any other way? Can't I help you to get out of this chimney?" said Tom.

"No," interposed the truncheon; "he has come to the place where everybody must help themselves; and he will find it out, I hope, before he is done with me."

"Oh, yes," said Grimes, "of course it's me. Did I ask to be

brought here into the prison? Did I ask to be set to sweep your foul chimneys? Did I ask to have lighted straw put under me to make me go up? Did I ask to stick fast in the very first chimney of all, because it was so shamefully clogged up with soot? Did I ask to stay here—I don't know how long—a hundred years, I do believe, and never get my pipe, nor my beer, nor nothing fit for a beast, let alone a man?"

"No," answered a solemn voice behind. "No more did Tom, when you behaved to him in the very same way."

It was Mrs. Bedonebyasyoudid. And, when the truncheon saw her, it started bolt upright—Attention!—and made such a low bow, that if it had not been full of the spirit of justice, it must have tumbled on its end, and probably hurt its one eye. And Tom made his bow too.

"Oh, ma'am," he said, "don't think about me; that's all past and gone, and good times and bad times and all times pass over. But may not I help poor Mr. Grimes? Mayn't I try and get some of these bricks away, that he may move his arms?"

"You may try, of course," she said.

So Tom pulled and tugged at the bricks: but he could not move one. And then he tried to wipe Mr. Grimes's face: but the soot would not come off.

"Oh, dear!" he said, "I have come all this way, through all these terrible places, to help you, and now I am of no use after all."

"You had best leave me alone," said Grimes; "you are a good-natured forgiving little chap, and that's truth: but you'd best be

off. The hail's coming on soon, and it will beat the eyes out of
your little head."

"What hail?"

"Why hail that falls every evening here; and, till it comes close
to me, it's like so much warm rain: but then it turns to hail over
my head, and knocks me about like small shot."

"That hail will never come any more," said the strange lady.
"I have told you before what it was. It was your mother's tears,
those which she shed when she prayed for you by her bedside;
but your cold heart froze it into hail. But she is gone to heaven
now, and will weep no more for her graceless son."

Then Grimes was silent a while; and then he looked very sad.

"So my old mother's gone, and I never there to speak to her!
Ah! a good woman she was, and might have been a happy one,
in her little school there in Vendale, if it hadn't been for me and
my bad ways."

"Did she keep the school in Vendale?" asked Tom. And then
he told Grimes all the story of his going to her house, and how
she could not abide the sight of a chimney-sweep, and then how
kind she was, and how he turned into a water-baby.

"Ah!" said Grimes, "good reason she had to hate the sight of a
chimney-sweep. I ran away from her and took up with the
sweeps, and never let her know where I was, nor sent her a penny
to help her, and now it's too late—too late!" said Mr. Grimes.

And he began crying and blubbering like a great baby, till his
pipe dropped out of his mouth, and broke all to bits.

"Oh dear, if I was but a little chap in Vendale again, to see the clear beck, and the apple-orchard, and the yew-hedge, how different I would go on! But it's too late now. So you go along, you kind little chap, and don't stand to look at a man crying, that's old enough to be your father, and never feared the face of man, nor of worse neither. But I'm beat now, and beat I must be. I've made my bed, and I must lie on it. Foul I would be, and foul I am, as an Irishwoman said to me once; and little I heeded it. It's all my own fault: but it's too late." And he cried so bitterly that Tom began crying too.

"Never too late," said the fairy, in such a strange soft new voice that Tom looked up at her; and she was so beautiful for the moment, that Tom half fancied she was her sister.

No more was it too late. For, as poor Grimes cried and blubbered on, his own tears did what his mother's could not do, and Tom's could not do, and nobody's on earth could do for him; for they washed the soot off his face and off his clothes; and then they washed the mortar away from between the bricks; and the chimney crumbled down; and Grimes began to get out of it.

Up jumped the truncheon, and was going to hit him on the crown a tremendous thump, and drive him down again like a cork into a bottle. But the strange lady put it aside.

"Will you obey if I give you a chance?"

"As you please, ma'am. You're stronger than me, that I know too well, and wiser than me, I know too well also. And, as for being my own master, I've fared ill enough with that as yet. So whatever your ladyship pleases to order me; for I'm beat, and that's the truth."

"Be it so then—you may come out. But remember, disobey me again, and into a worse place still you go."

"I beg pardon, ma'am, but I never disobeyed you that I know of. I never had the honour of setting eyes upon you till I came to these ugly quarters."

"Never saw me? Who said to you, Those that will be foul, foul they will be?"

Grimes looked up; and Tom looked up too; for the voice was that of the Irishwoman who met them the day that they went out together to Harthover. "I gave you your warning then: but you gave it yourself a thousand times before and since. Every bad word that you said—every cruel and mean thing that you did—every time that you got tipsy—every day that you went dirty—you were disobeying me, whether you knew it or not."

"If I'd only known, ma'am——"

"You knew well enough that you were disobeying something, though you did not know it was me. But come out and take your chance. Perhaps it may be your last."

So Grimes stepped out of the chimney, and, really, if it had not been for the scars on his face, he looked as clean and respectable as a master-sweep need look.

"Take him away," said she to the truncheon, "and give him his ticket-of-leave."

"And what is he to do, ma'am?"

"Get him to sweep out the crater of Etna; he will find some very steady men working out their time there, who will teach him his business: but mind, if that crater gets choked again, and there is an earthquake in consequence, bring them all to me, and I shall investigate the case very severely."

So the truncheon marched off Mr. Grimes, looking as meek as a drowned worm.

And for aught I know, or do not know, he is sweeping the crater of Etna to this very day.

"And now," said the fairy to Tom, "your work here is done. You may as well go back again."

"I should be glad enough to go," said Tom, "but how am I to get up that great hole again, now the steam has stopped blowing?"

"I will take you up the backstairs: but I must bandage your eyes first; for I never allow anybody to see those backstairs of mine."

"I am sure I shall not tell anybody about them, ma'am, if you bid me not."

"Aha! So you think, Tom. But you would soon forget your promise if you got back into the land-world. For, if people only once found out that you had been up my backstairs, you would have all the fine ladies kneeling to you, and the rich men emptying their purses before you, and statesmen offering you place and power; and young and old, rich and poor, crying to you, 'Only tell us the great backstairs secret, and we will be your slaves; we will make you lord, king, emperor, bishop, archbishop, pope, if you like—only tell us the secret of the backstairs.' So come—now I must bandage your eyes." So she tied the bandage on his eyes with one hand, and with the other she took it off.

"Now," she said, "you are safe up the stairs." Tom opened his eyes very wide, and his mouth too; for he had not, as he thought, moved a single step. But, when he looked round him, there could be no doubt that he was safe up the backstairs, whatsoever they may be, which no man is going to tell you, for the plain reason that no man knows.

The first thing which Tom saw was the black cedars, high and sharp against the rosy dawn; and St. Brandan's Isle reflected double in the still broad silver sea. The wind sang softly in the cedars, and the water sang among the caves; the sea-birds sang as they streamed out into the ocean, and the land-birds as they built among the boughs; and the air was so full of song that it stirred St. Brandan and his hermits, as they slumbered in the shade; and they moved their good old lips, and sang their morning hymn amid their dreams. But among all the songs one came across the water more sweet and clear than all; for it was the song of a young girl's voice.

And as Tom neared the island, there sat upon a rock the most graceful creature that ever was seen, looking down with her chin upon her hand, and paddling with her feet in the water. And when they came to her she looked up, and behold it was Ellie.

"Oh, Miss Ellie," said he, "how you are grown!"

"Oh, Tom," said she, "how you are grown, too!"

And no wonder; they were both grown up—he into a tall young man, and she into a beautiful young woman.

"Perhaps I may be grown," she said. "I have had the time; for I have been sitting here waiting for you many a hundred years, I thought you were never coming."

"Many a hundred years?" thought Tom; but he had seen so much in his travels that he had quite given up being astonished; and, indeed, he could think of nothing but Ellie. So he stood and looked at Ellie, and Ellie looked at him; and they liked the employment so much that they stood and looked for seven years more, and neither spoke nor stirred.

At last they heard the fairy say: "Attention, children! Are you never going to look at me again?"

"We have been looking at you all this while," they said. And so they thought they had been.

"Then look at me once more," said she.

They looked—and both of them cried out at once, "Oh, who are you, after all?"

"You are our dear Mrs. Doasyouwouldbedoneby."

"No, you are good Mrs. Bedonebyasyoudid; but you are grown quite beautiful now!"

"To you," said the fairy. "But look again."

"You are Mother Carey," said Tom, in a very low, solemn

voice; for he had found out something which made him very happy, and yet frightened him more than all that he had ever seen.

"But you are grown quite young again."

"To you," said the fairy. "Look again."

"You are the Irishwoman who met me the day I went to Harthover!"

And when they looked she was neither of them, and yet all of them at once.

"My name is written in my eyes, if you have eyes to see it there."

And they looked into her great, deep, soft eyes, and they changed again and again into every hue, as the light changes in a diamond.

"Now read my name," said she, at last.

And her eyes flashed, for one moment, clear, white, blazing light: but the children could not read her name; for they were dazzled, and hid their faces in their hands.

"Not yet, young things, not yet," said she, smiling; and then she turned to Ellie.

"You may take him home with you now on Sundays, Ellie. He has won his spurs in the great battle, and become fit to go with you and be a man; because he has done the thing he did not like."

So Tom went home with Ellie on Sundays, and sometimes on week-days, too; and he is now a great man of science, and can plan railroads, and steam-engines, and electric telegraphs, and rifled guns, and so forth; and knows everything about everything, except why a hen's egg doesn't turn into a crocodile, and two or three other little things which no one will know till the coming of the Cocqcigrues, when man shall be the measure of all things. And all this from what he had learned when he was a water-baby, underneath the sea.